I spun on my heel, running back toward camp, and my boss caught up with me at the perimeter of the guest tents. A white-coated helper stood outside the kitchen tent. He raised an arm, pointing to the far end of the encampment. Behind the last guest tent, we found them. Two men locked in an urgent embrace—one grizzled and frail and stretched out full length, the other robust and dark, cradling his companion across his knees.

Boyce found his voice first. "Who is it? What's happened?"

The kneeling man paused before answering. "It is Arkady Radishchev." A Russian. Or maybe two. The distinct Slavic accent explained his hesitation. "And he is dead."

"Dead? Are you sure?" I dropped to my knees beside them, ready to ride to the Russian's rescue. "Put him down so I can work on him."

I tossed a glance at my boss, who stood by, stiff and white-faced. "Boyce, call for medevac while I start CPR." That got him moving.

Way too slowly but oh-so-gently, the kneeling man lowered Arkady Radishchev to the ground. Then he withdrew hands smeared with blood and held them before me. "I am afraid my friend is beyond your help."

that she writes about her subject, with feeling and a wealth of fascinating detail."

"Lauren Maxwell is a detective for our times—an environmentalist, a feminist, and a single mother who balances catching the bad guys with grabbing quality time with the kids."

"*Murder Most Grizzly* offers some timely information and insights on the Alaskan ecology and introduces a likable and competent new female sleuth who's as passionate about the environment as about getting her man."

A Wolf in Death's Clothing

"The twists that Alaska's vastness works on the minds of the wary and unwary alike is the theme of this . . . second adventure for Lauren Maxwell, recovering widow, mother of two, and pistol-packin' private eye. . . . The solution lies in the clever application of Alaska lore."

"As the story weaves itself through the Alaskan expanse, its rivers and its mountains, its plants and its animals become characters in their own right. . . . Elizabeth Quinn's obvious love of the people and the land of Alaska is infectious."

Books by Elizabeth Quinn

Murder Most Grizzly
A Wolf in Death's Clothing
Lamb to the Slaughter

Published by POCKET BOOKS

For orders other than by individual consumers, Pocket Books grants a discount on the purchase of **10 or more** copies of single titles for special markets or premium use. For further details, please write to the Vice-President of Special Markets, Pocket Books, 1633 Broadway, New York, NY 10019-6785, 8th Floor.

For information on how individual consumers can place orders, please write to Mail Order Department, Simon & Schuster Inc., 200 Old Tappan Road, Old Tappan, NJ 07675.

LAMB TO THE SLAUGHTER

A LAUREN MAXWELL MYSTERY

ELIZABETH QUINN

POCKET BOOKS
New York   London   Toronto   Sydney   Tokyo   Singapore

This book is a work of fiction. Names, characters, places and incidents are products of the author's imagination or are used fictitiously. Any resemblance to actual events or locales or persons, living or dead, is entirely coincidental.

An *Original* Publication of POCKET BOOKS

POCKET BOOKS, a division of Simon & Schuster Inc.
1230 Avenue of the Americas, New York, NY 10020

Copyright © 1996 by Elizabeth Quinn Barnard

All rights reserved, including the right to reproduce this book or portions thereof in any form whatsoever. For information address Pocket Books, 1230 Avenue of the Americas, New York, NY 10020

ISBN: 0-671-52765-7

First Pocket Books printing October 1996

10 9 8 7 6 5 4 3 2 1

POCKET and colophon are registered trademarks of Simon & Schuster Inc.

Front cover illustration by Matthew Rotunda

Printed in the U.S.A.

In memory of John D. MacDonald
1916–1986
a master whose work showed me the way

The peaks are bright against the blue,
and drenched with sunset wine.

—*Robert Service*

LAMB TO THE SLAUGHTER

CHAPTER
1

Could any worse fate befall the reluctant hostess than having the guest of honor turn up dead on her doorstep? A couple of things, maybe. Like having her boss discover the body. Or having the deceased be an eminent Russian scientist of international reputation. And having the Russian's cause of death be murder. Final question: How in the hell does an obscure wildlife biologist get mixed up in murder—again?

That last question was the only one I could answer on the day it happened. The warm morning sun of early September dazzled across the mirrored waters of Wonder Lake, deep inside the national park that surrounds North America's highest mountain. Across the lake, a whirl of clouds shrouded Denali's peak but in no way diminished its grandeur. I've lived in the mountain's shadow for almost two decades, ever since my husband, Max, brought me to the Great Land, but Denali still pushes my pause button. That morning I stepped out of the large tent at the center of camp,

1

caught sight of the mountain looming over the lake and found myself transfixed.

"Lauren?" Coming close behind me, Boyce Reade dodged right to avoid a collision. "Anything wrong?"

In answer, I flung my arms wide, offering my boss the shimmering lake and the glowing autumn forest and the mountain radiant against a clear blue sky. And so he looked, too—for all of five seconds— before going right back to business. "Oh, yes. Very nice." He touched my arm to get me moving. "Let's start with the guest accommodations. The men are two to a tent, but you and Margaret Armstrong each have one of your own."

Business. That's what got me to Wonder Lake in time for murder. Each year my employer, the Wild America Society, sponsors an annual science conference, a meeting renowned for gourmet food in an exotic locale. This end-of-summer party is mostly a public relations gimmick, a chance for the ecowarriors to schmooze the scientists who provide most of our ammunition, because even the heavyweights in the enviro disciplines prefer to unveil breakthrough findings at their own professional meetings. Not that the Wild America shindig is total fluff. This year's agenda included three days focused on the controversial Gaia hypothesis and reserved the final day for an important international review of shelved research from the former Soviet Union. The fifty scientists on our guest list hailed from a dozen countries and included a handful of researchers with global reputations. For years I'd been wangling for an invitation to the Wild America conference, but my job as Alaska investigator was usually judged too removed—by geography and by content—to justify the transportation expense. Now that Wild America had finally sited the conference in my own backyard, I wanted no part of it. So far the high points of my summer had included standing fast when a grizzly charged me, avoiding panic when a killer hogtied me and drawing my own Colt .45 to subdue a creep who'd already gunned down two of my pals. After months of mayhem I needed a couple of solid weeks to rest, recharge my batteries and mommy my kids back home in Eagle River. What I did not need was another long weekend on the road, no matter how great the food or the company.

Fat chance. Any prospect of that had vanished two days earlier. The call came while Jessie and I were in my bathroom admiring our new haircuts in the triple mirror above my sink. I'd been working on her all summer, pointing out every cute, short cut I saw in movies, TV, photographs or real life and sighing deeply whenever called upon to comb, dry, curl or crimp her fine, straight hair. For thirty-five-plus years, I've been hair-challenged myself so imagine my growing horror as my little beauty grew into a saucy replica of myself, complete with laughing brown eyes, a front-tooth gap and poker straight brown hair. Hair nightmare squared! Not the color but the texture (fine) and the curl (zero). And, of course, Jessie wanted to wear her hair long. Below the shoulders, definitely, and below her butt, if possible. Mercifully, below the butt proved impossible, but below the shoulder was no problem. And there it was, Jessie's scraggly cascade of rich brown hair thinned to an uneven shag that draped around her eight-year-old shoulders. Getting myself to a hairdresser on a regular basis presented a major challenge in my too-busy life, but when the need arose, I could always avoid mirrors. Keeping my daughter's hair trimmed proved a more formidable challenge. I couldn't avoid her very well, and she objected to being locked in the closet. Jessie's older brother, Jake, had his own set of hair issues, but at twelve years old, he could be trusted to take a twenty-dollar bill, ride his bike to the barber and return home with most of the change and a not-too-horrifying haircut. Unfortunately, Jessie was still totally dependent on mom, whose months of careful groundwork had now borne fruit. She'd consented to a very short shelf cut that looked simply darling. I'd been so overcome with enthusiasm for my daughter's new look that I asked our hairdresser to suggest a makeover for me as well. I was admiring the results of her artistry with a razor, running my hands over the tightly cropped hair on the sides and back and finger-combing the slightly longer top, when the call came from Boyce.

Jessie dashed into my bedroom to pick up the telephone while I lingered in the bathroom for one last pat of my new coiffure. She answered with a chirp that quickly subsided into mournful tones. "Yeah. I'll get her."

When I followed her into the bedroom, she held the phone toward me and hissed in a stage whisper. "It's your boss." Her voice dropped a few decibels. "Do you have to go away again? You're not going to miss the camping trip, are you? You promised, Mom."

I took the phone from her, smothered it against my thigh and swung my free arm around her shoulders, pulling her close. "I don't think so, baby. I hope not." I glanced at the picture of Max on my bedside table, wondering for the bazillionth time why I'd been robbed of my mate and left to raise our children all alone. I gave Jessie a quick squeeze. "Let me find out what he wants, and then we'll figure out what has to be done."

I cocked the phone against my ear, wondering why my boss was still at Wild America headquarters in Washington, D.C., when he was supposed to be at our lakeside campsite at Denali Park. "Hey, Boyce, I thought you were up at Wonder Lake."

4

"I am. One of the rangers let me use their phone."
A short pause punctuated by a long sigh. "We have got
a real problem here."

His use of the word *we* was the tip-off. When your
boss tries to make his problem into our problem,
you're in trouble. Still hugging Jessie close, I sank
onto the bed. She craned her neck, trying to get an ear
into our conversation. "What's wrong?"

"Sally's dad fell and broke his hip. They've just
moved from Connecticut to someplace in Arizona—
few friends yet and obviously no family. She'll have to
go, of course. In fact, she's already left." Boyce's voice
held the faintest trace of irritation at the news of his
assistant's defection. I remembered that he'd been
through something similar when his elderly parents
decided to sell the family manse in Westchester
County and move to a golf-course development on an
island off the coast of Georgia. After less than a year
the Reades hated everything about the place—the
people, the climate, even the golf—and wanted their
own home back. "Which," he continued, "leaves me
without a hostess for the conference. Short notice, I
know, Lauren, but I'm really in a jam."

Another squeeze of Jessie's shoulder. "And what
does hostessing involve?"

"Mingling mostly. The scientists run their own
agenda. Plus you'd lead a few outings. Sally has
several scheduled. Offhand I recall only a short hike
to a new lake formed by a recent slide that dammed
up a creek."

"That sounds right up my alley." I shot a quick
glance down at Jessie's face. "How soon do you need
me?"

A bitter chuckle. "How soon can you get here? The
conferees arrive at midafternoon on Friday."

"I'll be on the last bus on Thursday evening. Square
that with the rangers, will you?"

After Boyce promised to handle the logistics at the Denali end of the connection, I hung up the phone and tried to square things at the Eagle River end. Flopping back onto the bed, I dragged my daughter with me and cuddled her against my side. "My boss needs help, Peanut, so I've got to go up to Denali Park for a few days. Just a couple. But I don't have to leave until late Thursday afternoon, so we still have a few days. And I'll be back late Wednesday night."

Jessie sat up and thrust out her chin. "Why do you have to go?" Her brown eyes shone with utter conviction. "Somebody else can do it. It doesn't have to be you."

"Not this time, sweetie. Remember Sally? The nice woman in Washington who sends you all that neat stuff from the White House and the Smithsonian?" For tone of voice I aimed at reasonable, in hopes that my daughter would respond in kind. Jessie's not usually a whiner and, from the time she could talk, has demonstrated a child's version of Solomon's wisdom. But she'd just returned from a three-week trip with friends to the Lower 48 and she really needed some serious Mommy time. "Well, Sally was all set to do it, but she's got big trouble at home."

And so I explained the problem to her in detail, and Jessie listened without interrupting. Behind those brown eyes, I could almost see the wheels spinning as she heard the evidence, examined the options and weighed the correctness of my course. She gets her capacity for reason and her precise logic from Max. Her daddy, a man she barely remembers, was killed in a plane crash several years ago. On the tough calls, Max never tried to duck a decision. Instead, he considered a problem with care and reached a conclusion. When he didn't know what to do, he said so. And when he made a decision, he stuck to it. His promises could be carved in stone. Jessie's too.

After I finished my explanation, Jessie sat for a few moments without speaking and then nodded. "You're right, Mom. You do have to go. But if you're coming back on Wednesday, can we still go camping next weekend?"

I brushed a quick kiss across her soft cheek. "I don't see why not."

Which is how I came to be at Wonder Lake in time for a six A.M. breakfast on Friday morning. Past the main visitor center, there's only one way in or out of Denali Park—shuttle buses provided by the National Park Service. Visitors can walk, of course, but few do. Boyce proved as good as his word, and I caught the last bus from the park headquarters on Thursday night, arriving at Wild America's camp eighty miles inside the park as the last of the long subarctic twilight faded to true dark. Jessie's determination to wring every last bit of fun from the two days between Boyce's call for help and my departure for Denali Park meant I arrived at Wonder Lake fit only for sleep. So my boss showed me to my tent, helped me spread out my sleeping bag and asked me to meet him for breakfast at six A.M. I didn't even hear the screen door shut behind him.

The next morning he breezed into the mess tent looking like his usual divine self. New strands of silver highlighted his dark mane of hair and new grooves crinkled around his rain-gray eyes, but such signs of maturity only heightened his appeal. Start with great looks and then add a superbly conditioned body, natural charm, a brilliant mind and you've got Boyce Reade—the thinking woman's beefcake. Not that I found him captivating right then. When he entered the tent, I stood up, but we'd barely exchanged good mornings before he succeeded in raising my hackles.

"What on earth possessed you to wear that . . . that . . ." A vague gesture in my direction left my cheeks burning. He didn't like my wardrobe? Talk about gall! His eyes sharpened on my midsection. "Is that a Colt .45?"

My hand dropped to the gun holstered on my hip. "Yeah." He didn't object to my wardrobe, just to my accessories! I unsnapped the holster and slid the .45 into my hand. "I carry this whenever I'm in the bush."

The gun lay across my palm, smooth and cool and awfully comforting after the summer I'd had. Boyce kept his distance but definitely looked the .45 over, the kind of careful examination usually reserved for weird specimens. After a few moments he raised his eyes to mine. "Do you really think it's necessary here?"

I resisted the urge to give the .45 a cowpoke spin around my trigger finger and slid the Colt back into the holster. "Does my carrying the gun bother you, Boyce?"

His eyes drifted from mine. "Frankly, yes."

And he hated to admit it. He probably expected a diatribe from me on gender, role models and sexist expectations. But I knew how difficult it was for him to admit this, and I did not think he deserved my scorn. Boyce Reade was one of the good guys, after all. When Sally asked for an emergency leave, he'd never considered any answer except yes, however disastrous the timing. He willingly put himself out to accommodate the needs of others. Which neatly fit my credo: Do the right thing. Now it was my turn.

I unbuckled the gunbelt. "No problem, boss." I brandished the holstered .45 in the direction of my tent. "Just let me tuck this cannon into my backpack. Then we'll have breakfast, and you can give me a tour."

By daylight, the Wild America camp turned out to be pretty amazing. And not just the great chow, including freshly baked croissants and real cappuccino. In addition to digging up a caterer who didn't balk at the notion of producing gourmet cuisine from a kitchen tent, my boss had also located an equipment rental firm that specialized in great-white-hunter camping gear—large canvas tents with mosquito-net "screen" doors, carpeted platform floors and safety-flued propane heaters. Boyce hadn't succeeded in persuading the park service that such deluxe digs were in keeping with guidelines for no-trace camping within Denali Park. "No-trace" means no trampled grass, no visible firepits, no litter, no nothing—not a realistic goal with our fifty-plus guests. He'd "settled" for making camp in the most coveted, lake-shore loop at the public campground.

From the kitchen and mess tents to the ring of canvas guest quarters and temporary showers, I gave the Wild America encampment a white-glove inspection. With the guests arriving in five hours, we wouldn't have time to smooth over any but the most minor glitches. Fortunately, even the park service bathrooms passed muster. As we walked, Boyce filled me in on the daily schedule and my role at the conference—mandatory appearances at meals and leading a daily outing. The obligatory campfire circle turned out to be the last stop on our tour. A double row of stump stools surrounded the rock-lined pit, about sixty in all, more than enough to accommodate the fifty scientists who'd be arriving later that morning. I had just settled myself on a stump stool to hear my boss's "one last thing" when a hoarse cry erupted, breaking the forest silence.

Boyce stiffened. "What was that?"

I spun on my heel, running back toward camp without answering. My boss caught up at the perimeter of the guest tents. A white-coated helper stood outside the kitchen tent. He raised an arm, pointing to the far end of the encampment. Behind the last guest tent, I found them. Two men locked in an urgent embrace—one grizzled and frail and stretched out full length; the other, robust and dark, cradling his companion across his knees.

Boyce found his voice first. "Who is it? What's happened?"

The kneeling man paused before answering. "It is Arkady Radishchev." A Russian. Or maybe two. The distinct Slavic accent explained his hesitation. "And he is dead."

"Dead? Are you sure?" I dropped to my knees beside them, ready to ride to the Russian's rescue. "Put him down so I can work on him."

I tossed a glance at my boss who stood by, stiff and white-faced. "Boyce, call for medevac while I start CPR." That got him moving.

Way too slowly but oh-so-gently, the kneeling man lowered Arkady Radishchev to the ground. Then he withdrew hands smeared with blood and held them before me. "I am afraid my friend is beyond your help."

NOT A CHANCE. FROM A DISTANCE, reviving the dead man seemed possible. Up close, the utter stillness of the corpse proved that the Russian truly was beyond my help. The action of gravity had pooled the blood, draining the flush of life from his skin and leaving his face a white transparency pierced by empty eyes. I nudged the heavy lids closed and turned my attention to the living.

Except for breathing, the dead man's friend hadn't moved. He stared at his upraised hands as the warm September air dried the blood. On impulse I reached out, enclosing his bloody hands within my own. "Tell me what happened."

For a moment his stare focused on our entwined hands. Then he lifted his head and fixed his green eyes on my face. "Who are you?"

That flustered me. I drawled out a lame introduction—name, affiliation, scientific specialty—in the slow speech and careful pronunciation Americans reserve for annoying children and authentic foreigners, all the while nodding my head and squeezing his bloody hands. The dead man's friend humored me, gently extracting himself from my grip before returning the introduction. He turned out to be a botanist named Konstantin Zorich from a world-class laboratory located in darkest Siberia. The dead man turned out to be the director of the illustrious institute, a very big mucky-muck and our guest of honor.

My stomach cramped as I glanced down at the body, and my words came out in a squeak. *"The* Arkady Radishchev?"

Konstantin Zorich rescued me with laughter that originated deep in his belly and built into an impressive roar. "This he would love."

I gave him an uncertain smile. He still hadn't told me what happened, but the presence of so much blood definitely pointed to an unnatural cause of death.

His arms flailed in time with the eruption of laughter. "The Americans are knowing him."

Of course we know him. Why else would Wild America invite him to keynote our conference? I eyed the other visiting Russian.

Konstantin Zorich's laughter subsided as quickly as it began. He clamped one large bloody hand around his friend's lifeless arm. "Oh, Arkady, all these years have we wondered, only for me to find out now." He shook his head, setting his shag of dark curls dancing. "And for you, my friend, too late."

On that solemn note, Boyce Reade trotted back, followed by a chef's helper toting a first-aid kit emblazoned with a red cross. "Too late?" His eyes swung around to meet mine. "Lauren, are you sure?"

I nodded and let out a sigh. "I'm sure. He's been

dead for a while." I sat back on my heels. "This could be trouble. I mean, this guy's a pretty big name."

My boss raised his eyebrows. "Arkady Radishchev? Quite."

"I don't think you get it, Boyce." I grabbed one of Zorich's bloody hands and waved it at my boss. "This was no natural death."

At times, Boyce's control seems bred in the bone, but at my pronouncement, his nostrils flared, as if reacting to a foul and unexpected odor. His glance flicked to me, to Konstantin Zorich and to the dead Russian before settling on the young chef's helper standing open-mouthed beside him. "Looks like we're too late for first aid, young man. But my thanks for your quick response." He gave the boy's shoulder a brisk squeeze that nudged him firmly in the direction of the kitchen tent. "Time now to return to your duties."

Underneath the sugar-coating of charm and good manners, the order rang clear: Dismissed! Before leaving, the boy threw one last look over his shoulder. I fought the urge to shout "Wait up!" and charge after him. At that moment I couldn't imagine a finer way to spend the day than peeling bushels of fresh vegetables and stirring vats of delicate sauces. I longed for the sanity of hearth and home, the dull everydayness of cooking breakfast. Right about now my kids would be waking up. In my absence, my housemate, Nina, would roust them before leaving for the veterinary office she used to share with Max, undoubtedly sweetening the wake-up call with the news that she'd left pancakes warming in the oven. Jessie would be the first to the table—breakfast is her favorite meal. Jake likes to take his time getting up and would probably detour outside to toss some fish to Esther, the otter who's lived in our creek since a friend rescued her near the Kuskokwim River. Rescue was what I wanted at that moment. The summer that began with madness and proceeded to mayhem had now ended in death. I craved rest but wound up with a rematch instead.

Having cleared the kitchen help from the scene, Boyce turned his attention to our guests—living and dead. First, he shrugged out of his Pendleton shirt and spread the plaid wool over the head and shoulders of Arkady Radishchev. Then he laid a firm hand on Konstantin Zorich's arm. "I expect you'd like to clean up."

He inclined his head in my direction and flashed a stern glance that warned me not to argue. "Lauren, here, will provide escort and keep you company until we get this sorted out."

After standing guard while the Russian washed up in the nearest bathroom, I detoured my charge past the bar cart in the mess tent and let him choose his own bracer. Without hesitation, he plucked a bottle of Jack Daniel's off the shelf. As he led me to his tent at the lake end of camp, I wondered why Boyce hadn't mentioned the early arrival of the Russians. In the shadowed interior of the tent, we settled in for a long day.

Konstantin Zorich chose one of the narrow beds, mounding two pillows before stretching out full length, the whiskey bottle cradled on his chest. The worn and much-mended duffel bag under the other bed signaled Arkady Radishchev's earlier claim, and somehow I couldn't cozy up to a dead man's bed. Instead, I positioned myself midway between the Russian and the door on the straight-backed wooden chair that matched the campaign table which completed the outfitting of our guest tents. Scientists are scribblers, after all, or so Boyce figured. However, the campaign table in my tent held not scholarly papers but my makeup kit, Discman and CDs, the paperback I was currently reading, 35mm camera and Colt .45-caliber automatic. And there was no evidence of academia or consumption cluttering the Russian's campaign table either. The dust-free surface shone in the midmorning light.

My charge made no conversation. For the first half hour, he simply stared straight ahead, even when tilting a swallow of whiskey into his mouth. He'd drained an inch by the time his eyes closed. When his drinking and his breathing had slowed enough to suggest sleep, I retrieved the Jack Daniel's, screwed on the cap and resumed my post.

Konstantin Zorich didn't fit my notion of Russian. Not that I've met too many. Still, I had a firm mental image of Russian males as fleshy-faced, barrel-chested, poorly dressed and smelling faintly of cabbage. I suppose that impression derived from the spy novels I read. (LeCarre is my favorite.) The Russian sleeping on the cot before me didn't look at all like one of the bad guys. The dark curl draped across his forehead in a cartoon of innocence softened a rugged face that featured about forty years' worth of squint and smile lines, a not-bad nose with a slight bump that implied a painful past and a shadow of manly stubble spreading across lean sun-darkened cheeks. Nice. Very nice. He lacked the barrel chest and odor of cabbage of my imagination, and his clothes, while showing definite signs of wear, looked well made and well cared for. A pullover in a dark blue knit snugged his broad shoulders and wide chest, and the corduroy pants boasted a carefully mended patch on the left knee. The real surprise was his calf-length leather boots—well broken in but displaying the soft gleam of a recent buffing with saddle soap. From my reading,

I'd supposed all Russians wore cheap plastic shoes. Maybe this fellow wasn't your typical Russian. After all, he certainly didn't fit my stereotype. I wondered again how he'd gotten to Wonder Lake before all the other conferees, and what kind of accident his friend had met with to produce so much blood?

His friend, Arkady Radishchev, was a legitimate scientific superstar. Celebrated in the West in the bad old Soviet days for fiercely independent thought, he'd emerged at home in these brave new days as an authentic Russian hero. But even when the iron hand of group thought had ruled his homeland, the bad guys hadn't gone around knocking off mavericks like Radishchev. Remember Andrei Sakharov and Yelena Bonner? Even in the days of communism, the U.S.S.R. employed decidedly capitalistic weapons against unmanageable scientists—character assassination, funding freezes and rumors of lunacy. Poor Arkady Radishchev had survived all of that and worse, only to die on his first trip to the U.S. Except that the dead Russian obviously wasn't a tourist gunned down at random for his vacation bankroll. Your big spenders generally avoid international scientific gatherings, after all. But no matter the cause of death, he was definitely dead, a fact that was not likely to inspire much confidence in the other scientists on our guest list.

Take for instance, Lawrence Cameron, a big-name theorist from our nation's capital whose most famous hypothesis was the nominal subject of our conference. In a word—*Gaia*. Like all scientists, Cameron's theorizing began with a *how come?* Of the three planets closest to the sun, how come Venus is too hot for life and Mars is too cold for life but Earth is just right? "Just lucky" *was* the correct answer for the longest time. But Cameron forced a reexamination by noting that when life began on Earth 3.8 million years ago, our sun burned cooler and dimmer. Today the sun emits twenty-five percent more light and heat, but our planet's average temperature remains a comfortable fifty-nine degrees Fahrenheit. Which is nineteen percent cooler than Earth's seventy-three degrees average temperature when life began. How come the planet is cooler even though the sun is hotter and brighter? Cameron's Gaia hypothesis posits that the Earth acts like a giant living organism, with all living things interacting to maintain the stability required by life, including stable temperatures. Call it brilliant or call it bullshit, Cameron's Gaia hypothesis definitely incites argument whenever the subject comes up.

The subject of Gaia always comes up with biologist Margaret Armstrong on hand. The biggest female name on our guest list, Armstrong extended Cameron's Gaia hypothesis and simultaneously stood the venerable Charles Darwin on his antique head. Forget survival of the fittest, Armstrong said, forget evolution powered by natural selection. The symbiosis implicit in Gaian interaction is the true engine of evolution—those living organisms that get along also go along, and those that don't, don't. In the church of Darwin, such heresy brings down ringing denunciations from the high priests of zoology.

A leading acolyte in Darwin's church, Thomas B. Hart, was also scheduled to attend the Wild America conference and, from all accounts, could be counted on to play the devil's advocate on the subject of Gaia. A prolific popularizer with a regular column in one of the most popular science magazines, he objected to Cameron's Gaia hypothesis for two reasons. First, Hart asserted, the Earth's inability to reproduce means the planet can't be "alive." And, in addition, how would the species interact to regulate the planet's environment—by committee, congress or parliament? But despite Hart's objections to Gaia, the hypothesis was catching on, and the buzz in the scientific community included the word that the popularity of Cameron's hypothesis really ticked him off. So much so, in fact, that what was once a warm friendship had cooled to frigid enmity.

The chance to rekindle an old friendship provided the only plus in my last-minute summons to the Wild America conference at Wonder Lake. Among the conferees scheduled to attend was an old grad-school chum named Jack McIntire. He'd been a year or two ahead of me at Berkeley, a botanist whose greatest gift seemed to be a green thumb that nurtured the sapling scholars contending for the limited nourishment available in the forest of biology. Once or twice I'd been discouraged enough to consider quitting until Jack bucked me up with kind words and a supportive shoulder. That kind of friendship can never grow cold.

The early morning chatter of birds had subsided and the sun had burned the mist off the lake before Boyce reappeared. I'd almost decided to abandon my post and go look for my boss when he rounded the lake end of the tent encampment and headed my way. I snuck a quick glance at Konstantin Zorich, and my heart lurched. Two slick trails of tears leaked from his still-closed eyes. So silent, so still but grieving, not sleeping. He'd retreated into himself to mourn his friend.

I stepped out of the shadowed tent and into the brilliant sunshine to meet Boyce, wondering if the frown on my face matched the severity of his. I don't mind aging, but I prefer laugh lines.

"The ranger just got here." Boyce tossed a glance toward the Russian's tent. "Murder's his bailiwick."

Another lurch of my heart. "Murder? Are you sure?"

"Looks like murder. Weapon's definitely a gun, probably a big one." He put a hand on my shoulder. "And the ranger wants to start his investigation by seeing yours."

CHAPTER
3

Somebody's dead and a cop wants to see your gun. You can be innocent as hell and still find that news unnerving. Forget that I had an alibi witness. Forget that the "cop" in this case was really a park ranger. *Ranger* rhymes with *danger,* which is exactly what I felt when Boyce Reade told me about my gun—in danger. A shot of adrenaline hit my bloodstream, ratcheting up the rate of my heartbeat and respiration, leaving me jittery and poised for flight or fight. I shrugged my boss's hand off my shoulder and sidestepped to a safe distance. "You've got to be kidding?"

"Not in the least."

"Then *he's* kidding." The words came out way too loud, so I modulated down to a hiss. "Maybe the Russian was shot but not with my gun. And how did the ranger hear about it, anyway?"

"I told him, Lauren." Boyce used his silkiest handle-with-care voice, gentling the frightened creature. Me. "He asked if there were any guns in camp, so I told him about yours."

I spun on my heel and walked a few steps toward the lake. Shit—they wanted to see my gun. My gun couldn't be the murder weapon. Could it?

Boyce came up behind me and risked putting his hand on my shoulder again. "I'm certain this is all purely routine. You haven't done anything, Lauren. You have nothing to fear."

I snorted and scuffed my foot in the dust. Tell that to the guy in Texas who spent ten years in prison for a robbery he didn't commit. People who haven't done anything get screwed all the time.

Boyce's fingers gently closed over my shoulder. "Let's not make him unhappy, Lauren. He'll get to see your gun in the end, anyway. Don't give him a reason to think you've got something to hide."

Way off across the lake, Denali stood rock-solid and unyielding and yet somehow comforting to one who loved the mountain. I had nothing to hide, but I was still damned scared. If unexplained deaths are spooky, then murder's terrifying. Where was I when Arkady Radishchev met his death? Asleep in my tent? Munching a gourmet breakfast? I hadn't heard anything, I hadn't seen anything, I didn't know anything. But I owned a gun, one the cops wanted to see. And irrational as it may seem, I found that news pretty scary. After taking a deep cleansing breath, I turned back to my boss. "Let's just get it over with."

He inclined his head toward the tent. "The ranger also wants to see the surviving Russian. Name's Zorich, correct?"

I nodded. "Konstantin Zorich." Details don't escape Boyce Reade, at least none having to do with the Wild America Society. He's a true believer in the cause and in Wild America. "He's a botanist and a protégé of Radishchev."

After giving fair warning with a chorus of throat-clearing, we entered the tent and roused the grieving Russian from his cot. Not that Konstantin Zorich seemed ashamed of his weeping. He sat up and heard Boyce out before even raising a hand to wipe the tears from his cheeks. After the explanation, he stood, dug a hand into a pocket of his worn corduroys and came up with a handkerchief, pristine, white and even ironed! To a woman born to the world of Kleenex and permanent press, that accessory seemed a charming throwback to a slower and possibly finer world. So did the shameless weeping. How many American men do you know who're willing to show a tear-streaked face to complete strangers? Counting my late husband, I knew maybe six, tops. And all of them taken. Including, it seemed, Konstantin Zorich—snagged by a lady willing to iron his hankies.

After detouring through my own tent to pick up my .45, I joined the men in the mess tent, pausing just inside the screen door to let my eyes adjust to the shadowy interior. Even before Albert Coppola motioned me forward, I recognized Denali's chief ranger from photos in the park's newsletter—bulldog jaw, brush-cut white bristle, shrewd but laughing eyes. No laughter in those blue eyes today. Also—thankfully—no menace.

He popped a fresh Zip-loc bag from a box at his elbow and opened the gallon-size wide before offering it to me. "Put your weapon in here, Mrs. Maxwell. Can you ease the gun out of the holster with just your fingertips?"

"Call me Lauren. Please."

From his seat across the table, Konstantin Zorich watched the exchange closely. I managed to slide the Colt from the holster into the bag without touching metal. After which the Russian's gaze slowly drifted over me, almost as if sizing me up. Had he seen one-too-many Hollywood-import *femmes fatales?* Not that he looked scared. In fact, when his gaze finally reached my face, he didn't look intimidated or intrigued—just sympathetic.

"Take a seat, Lauren, and we'll get started." Albert Coppola pointed to the empty director's chair next to Konstantin Zorich and then waited until I got myself into it before getting down to business. When I'd settled myself sufficiently, he pulled a small tape recorder out of his jacket pocket and raised the machine for all to see. "This talk may seem informal, but it is official and I'm getting it all on tape."

After positioning the machine on the table in front of us, he leaned toward the Russian. "Your name is Konstantin Zorich?"

Our guest straightened his shoulders and looked directly at the park ranger. "That is correct."

Coppola nodded and ran a hand over the bristle of his flat-top. "And you make your home in Magadan, which is in Siberia?"

"Yes, but not quite." Zorich crossed his arms and leaned forward onto the table, eyes never wavering from his questioner. "The institute receives mail through an address in Magadan, that is true. But the . . . the . . . how do you say? . . . The place of our buildings is not in the city. We are away to the north in the countryside."

"Far?"

Zorich nodded. "Yes. Far."

Coppola raised an eyebrow. "How far?"

"Many kilometers." The Russian lifted his shoulders into a shrug. "Perhaps seventy-five."

Coppola tugged his ear. "Seventy-five kilometers. Wonder what that is in miles?"

I jumped right in with the answer. "Just short of forty-seven."

Boyce raised an eyebrow, and Albert Coppola

23

flashed me a quick smile. "Thank you, Lauren. Now what about this phone number you gave me? That ring in the city, too?"

"No, no, no." A hint of color washed up the Russian's neck. "That telephone is ringing on my desk. In my office. And also my home." The flush deepened into a definite red. "The institute is also my home. Where I am working is also where I am living."

"Sounds like my place in Eagle River." Again I ignored Boyce's eyebrows. I don't mind seeing a grown man cry, but obvious embarrassment always leaves me feeling small. I can't resist riding to the rescue. "Lots of Americans work out of their homes, especially in Alaska."

Konstantin Zorich dipped his head in my direction. "Many Russians live in their workplace, especially in Siberia."

I would imagine that the first visit to the U.S. can be overwhelming, even a trip to the last frontier. Not the mountains, mind you, but the excess. Of everything. We have so much. Cars, bikes, boats, skis, airplanes, snow machines, motorcycles, three-wheelers and RVs up the wazoo. And that's just the toys. Need some new jeans? Try the department store, the specialty shop, the discount house, the boutique, or maybe just leaf through the millions of catalogs that arrived last week in the mail. A friend of mine complains about having too many choices. He needed a weed-whacker but left the hardware store without buying because choosing from the dozen displayed just stressed him out. And how about all the new megamarkets for food? I dropped by Safeway recently with a visitor from China, who observed on the diet-food aisle, "In my country, we wonder how to feed a billion people. In your country, you wonder how to eat more but weigh less." Talk about embarrassed.

Took me a week to look at an apple without feeling guilty.

As the interview continued, my mind drifted a bit, only vaguely recording what I heard—departures from Russia, arrivals in the U.S., sightseeing in Anchorage, consultations in Fairbanks. Since the Russians had planned an itinerary beyond the Wild America conference, they'd been on their own getting to Denali Park. Which explained how they managed to arrive before everybody else. Getting to the headquarters of Denali National Park is easy. But getting from there to the Wild America encampment at Wonder Lake, eighty-five miles down the road, can be pretty difficult since the park shuttle buses are first-come-first-served and fill up fast. That's why I'd asked Boyce to pull some strings and reserve me a spot on the last bus the night before. And that's why I perked my ears when Coppola finally got around to the shuttle.

"You say you came in yesterday? Rode the last bus from park headquarters?"

Zorich nodded vigorously, but I knew that couldn't be. I'd ridden the last packed bus from park headquarters, arriving breathless at the shuttle stop after leaving the 4-Runner in a distant lot and jogging all the way back with a gearbag slung from each shoulder. Boyce had come through with a reserved seat right behind the driver. As soon as I collapsed into the seat, the little yellow school bus rolled onto Denali Park's one road. By the time we reached the Savage River campground just before milepost thirteen, I was having trouble keeping my eyes open, and long before we reached Polychrome Pass around milepost fifty, I'd dug my pillow out of a bag and given in to exhaustion. I slept straight through the stop at the Eielson Visitor Center at milepost sixty-six, but I somehow managed to rouse myself for our arrival at Wonder Lake. Despite my pride of place at the front of the bus, I'd been the last one off. Meaning I'd watched every other rider negotiate the narrow aisle and steps; Konstantin Zorich hadn't been among them.

I glanced at Boyce. His eyebrows had risen again, and I realized that he, too, knew Zorich was lying. Boyce had met my bus when it arrived at Wonder Lake and knew as well as I did that neither Zorich nor his late friend rode that shuttle.

Before I could figure out what to do about Zorich's lie, Coppola prodded the Russian into another clumsy revelation. "So you took the last shuttle and got off here in Wonder Lake."

"Yes, but also no." Again Zorich shrugged. "Yes, my friend and I are riding last bus. But we are not exiting here. We are exiting at the center for visitors."

This time Albert Coppola's eyebrows arched to match Boyce's, and my own twitched in disbelief. Probably all shared the same thought, wondering how the Russians managed to cover the nineteen miles between the Eielson Visitor Center and our campground, and arrive in time for Arkady Radishchev's death?

Zorich had a simple explanation. "We are walking."

"You walked nineteen miles? When did you find the time?"

"Last night." For a second, the Russian paused, smiling slightly as he scanned our faces. "Through the night we are walking. Such soft air. Such brilliant stars. And all around the great mountains glowing with moonlight. We are walking through the night, and morning finds us here, at this lake."

Maybe Konstantin Zorich's smile had magic. His explanation sounded crazy, but I believed him. Truth be told, after taking my seat in the front of the bus without even glancing at the rest of the passengers, I'd slept most of the way from park headquarters. My mother could have been on that bus, and I wouldn't have noticed. If pressed, I could probably swear who got off at Wonder Lake, but in good conscience I'd have to demur if asked who was on the bus at park headquarters or anywhere in between.

Zorich's smile infected everyone in that tent, spreading from me to Boyce and finally to Albert Coppola, a clean sweep of smiles that soon widened into grins. From stone faces to gargoyles in an instant, no longer than it takes to strike a match. For the three acolytes of Wild America in that mess tent, the Russian's moonlit walk proved that Konstantin Zorich was okay. He was one of our kind.

CHAPTER
4

DISSOLVING MY SMILE TOOK SOME DO-
ing, but Boyce Reade managed the meltdown. After
inserting a pause in the proceedings with a perfectly
timed throat-clearing, he explained to the ranger that
our busload of conferees had probably just arrived
and guessed we should get over to the shuttle stop to
greet them. Then, after exchanging nods with the
chief ranger and Konstantin Zorich, he grabbed my
elbow and steered me out of the mess tent.

As soon as the screen door banged shut behind us, I
gently tugged my elbow free. "The bus isn't due for
another fifteen minutes, and I bet Albert Coppola
knows that."

Boyce kept walking, and I had to trot to catch him
and his words. "I don't believe that a man in Coppola's position clutters his mind with trivialities like
shuttle schedules."

"Boy, are you out of it!" I fell into step beside him,
matching my stride with his. "Visitor services are the
main preoccupation at all of our national parks,

which is why they're all going to hell. At Denali, accessibility is the biggest issue. I bet Coppola designed the bus schedule. I know he spends a lot of time defending it."

Boyce nudged my arm, turning me away from the ring of tents and toward the lake. "Let's spend the little time we have figuring out what to tell our guests about this morning's mishap."

That's when the first crack appeared in my smile. "Mishap? You call what happened to Arkady Radishchev a *mishap?*"

He angled toward the circle of stumps ringing the fire pit. "What do you suggest we call it?"

"*Murder* would be my suggestion. You said so yourself."

Boyce stopped in front of one of the stumps and waved me to a seat before taking his own. "I said Radishchev's death, and I quote, 'looks like murder.'" He leveled steady gray eyes upon my face. "Although the line is sometimes rather fine, there is a difference between how things appear and how they actually are. Witness Zorich's explanation of their early arrival at Wonder Lake. Initially, we both thought he was lying because we both knew he hadn't ridden that last shuttle. But, of course, he had—just not to Wonder Lake."

I leaned toward him. "Do you think he's responsible for Arkady Radishchev's death?"

"Not a chance."

The answer came so quickly, almost automatically, that I felt a tinge of outrage, even though my boss's certainty agreed with my own gut feeling. "Why not?"

Boyce shrugged. "Killing Arkady Radishchev would be like killing Copernicus or Galileo. He was a bona fide scientific hero. He faced down the communist crackpots and never blinked." He spread his hands. "Why do you think such an eminent scientist was out in God-knows-where Siberia? The Soviet term was 'enemy of the state.'"

When I admitted the sketchiness of my knowledge, Boyce filled me in on the recent history of Soviet science. Turned out much of it happened before my time, which explained why I had only a vague notion of the havoc wrought on Russian genetics by Trofim Lysenko, a crackpot to rival the infamous Chevalier de Lamarck, who believed adaptations to environment could be inherited. Lysenko took Lamarck and added a Marxist spin. After all, if changes to the environment did not result in changes to the species, how would the U.S.S.R. ever produce the New Man that Marx predicted? Talk about being blinded by politics! For many decades, communist ideology buried genetic fact. Poor old Gregor Mendel must have spun in his grave! In the bad old Soviet days, a lot of good scientists fearing the grave renounced the indisputable facts of genetic inheritance, but not Arkady Radishchev.

"That's why neither Zorich nor any other Russian would have killed him. In a time with few heroes, Radishchev stands out."

That also explained why Arkady Radishchev had been chosen by the new Russian government to lead a series of reviews of laboratory archives from the bad old Soviet days with an eye toward rescuing good science that had been shelved for ideological reasons. The first review session was scheduled for the concluding day of our Gaia conference, but now the kickoff would have to be postponed. Not Wild America's problem, thank God. That thought warmed me a bit, as did Boyce Reade's certainty of Konstantin Zorich's innocence.

After crossing my legs and locking hands around one knee, I took a moment to breathe in a lungful of spruce-fragrant air and admire the flight of a golden eagle that swooped low along the water's edge, but Boyce soon interrupted my reverie. "What should we tell our guests?"

I dropped my knee and leaned toward him again. "Lord knows I'm no girl scout, but telling the truth is always best. Straight, unvarnished truth may wound, but at least the cut's clean and heals quickly. Trying to shade the story or get the right spin just mucks things up, and the wound festers."

He raised an eyebrow. "And what is the truth about Arkady Radishchev's death?"

Meltdown! The fact that Boyce wanted my opinion had firmed up my smile, but the whole thing collapsed in the face of his impossible question. The only truth I could swear to was the fact of the Russian's death. I'd seen the body, after all, and you didn't need a Ph.D. to figure out that Arkady Radishchev was dead. But figuring out all the rest—the *how,* the *when,* the *why* and, if data supported a determination of murder, even the *who*—required way more information than I had at that moment.

"I see your point. We really don't know what happened. So maybe we should just stick to the facts: Arkady Radishchev is dead and may have been murdered."

A tongue of cool air wafted in from the lake, and he smoothed the front of the flannel shirt that had replaced the Pendleton wool he'd spread over Arkady Radishchev's bloodless face. "Do you think that's enough? Will they accept our explanation and carry on?"

"They might if we open the bar immediately. That'll get them over the initial shock." I ticked off my suggestions on my fingers. "Follow the extended happy hour with a sumptuous meal and a good night's sleep, and they may be fine tomorrow."

A rising tide of confidence buoyed my spirits.

Maybe the conference could still succeed. Maybe it wasn't murder, after all. "It's not like the Russian was a pal to anybody except Zorich. No way he's going anywhere soon. And the rest can't just pack up and go home. This is still the Alaskan bush."

"So you expect the alcohol will soothe any early jitters, and by morning they'll be worry-free?"

I glanced at my watch and then stood up. The bus should be heading into camp right now. "Sure. What's there to worry about?"

Boyce rose to his feet. "Close proximity to a clever killer?"

My lungs froze up for just a second, leaving me strangling on reassuring words. Talk about your switcheroos. Seemed like we'd traded attitudes—I'd eased into his blasé one while he now labored under my anxiety. And neither of us could afford any doubts if we were to pull this thing off. Time to buck up the troops.

"Clever killer? You must be joking." I resurrected my smile and gave one of his broad shoulders a reassuring pat. "Denali Park's a dead end—only one way in or out unless you figure on climbing the Alaska Range. Not what I'd call a clever location for staging a murder."

To the east, the thrum of an engine grew louder, and Boyce turned in that direction. "That's one way of looking at it."

I threaded through the stumps and headed for the shuttle stop, tossing a final challenge over my shoulder. "Give me another."

For a second, I heard nothing but the scuff of his boots against the hard-packed dirt of a well-used trail. When he spoke again, his voice was soft and low, an uneasy murmur that lingered in my mind long after his voice faded from my ears. "Perhaps he'll stay.

Since he can't escape without notice, perhaps he never meant to try. Instead he'll hide among us until we all go. And then he'll slip away."

Yellow showed through the screen of trees as the classic all-American school bus used to shuttle visitors through Denali Park came into sight. I quickened my pace and tried to push Boyce's gloomy words out of my mind. Not counting Boyce or myself, "us" consisted of a couple dozen world-class scientists, hardly an easy group for a murderer to get lost within. Unless he belonged to the group. And that made no sense because they were only just arriving. If neither Boyce, Zorich, the new arrivals nor I had harmed Radishchev, that left no practical suspect among "us." And that easily I stuffed Boyce Reade's gloomy murmur into a very deep hole, succeeding in burying his speculation. For a while, at least.

Up ahead, passengers piled off the bus and formed a half circle around the open door. As we approached the road, I scanned the knot of bystanders for Jack McIntire's familiar face but didn't find him among the crowd, a milling swarm of fifty or so of the best scientific minds of several generations. When we reached the gravel road, an angular woman with sturdy boots and cropped gray hair spotted us and called out Boyce's name. He moved ahead of me just as the herd of scientists turned in our direction. All except for one thin fellow who stood a little apart from the group, staring at the spectacular peak that rose so far above the waters of Wonder Lake.

Like a well-trained camp counselor, I moved in his direction, ready to shoo my wandering charge back to the main group. More lean than thin, I decided upon further consideration, with a shock of red hair thickly streaked with gray and bright blue eyes that seemed reluctant to trade the sight of my ordinary features for that natural grandeur. "Looks like the mountain's got its hooks into you. The Athabascans called it Denali, 'The High One,' but they never climbed it."

"Of course not. Such places are for the gods, not mere mortals." He spoke with the trace of a Southern accent and raised his arm to point across the lake. "And that great wall of stone that we passed? What do they call that?"

"You must mean the Wickersham Wall. A granite face. Most of the Alaska Range is granite."

"Yes, but The High One's composition is a bit different than these other peaks, granite a bit lighter." He lifted his hands in front of us, gently waving them back and forth. "And so your Denali floats just that much higher on the magma core, rises just that much higher on the surface."

Before I could respond, he clapped his hands together and turned to face me. "And up rises that Wickersham Wall, a great blade splitting the plate from below." He chopped upward with both hands and then spread his fingers to knead the air. "A blade that churns the center of the earth, releasing trapped minerals to freshen the biosphere above." His smile lit those pale blue eyes. "Marvelous! Just marvelous!"

I opened my mouth to speak, but he got in ahead of me again. "The Wickersham Wall is Gaia unfolding, changes visible not in my lifetime or yours, perhaps not even in a millennium. Ever so slowly Gaia unfolds, stirring her brews—her atmosphere, her oceans, her melting core below." He snatched at the air before him. "Producing, consuming, exchanging, replenishing, on and on it goes—Gaia unfolding, life evolving."

He paused at last, leaving me free to speak but suddenly without words. I fell back on common courtesy, offering him my hand. "I'm Lauren Maxwell, of the Wild America Society."

He took my hand firmly for one vigorous shake. "And I am Lawrence Cameron."

The Man! I should have guessed. Probably standing off by himself because no one else had the chutzpah to approach him. Every other scientist at our conference came with a citation attached to his address in an appendix of our schedule of events, a paragraph detailing that Dr. Big Shot, followed by a lengthy string of abbreviated degrees, held the Quack Quack McHuey Chair in Physical Sciences at the Hard Knocks School of International Rocks at the University of Cutting Edge Nerddom. Everybody but the Man, that is. Lawrence Cameron presented himself quite simply—name, address at a university in Washington, D.C., and even a home telephone number. For the heavyweights of science, Cameron's name was enough. Those who required more than his name obviously were out of it. For some reason, I felt absurdly pleased to be in the know and a bit let down when he dropped my hand after one perfunctory shake.

"Cameron! There you are." The woman in the leather hiking boots trotted over to us with Boyce hard on her heels. "Don't you dare wander off alone in this wilderness. Something nasty might eat you, and that would never do." The glint of affection in her dark eyes softened her words, and she moved aside to allow Boyce into our circle. "Meet Boyce Reade of Wild America. This is his shindig."

The men exchanged handshakes and greetings, then Lawrence Cameron raised a hand in my direction. "And you, my dear Margaret, must meet Lauren Maxwell, also of Wild America."

I was so flattered that the great man remembered my name that I nearly missed Margaret Armstrong's emphatic "Hah!" Fortunately, I caught the exclamation, which almost sent me into the stratosphere. Not only had Lawrence Cameron remembered my name, but his brilliant colleague seemed to know me already. I hadn't a clue how, but the great lady soon solved that little mystery.

"I'm looking forward to our outings." She grabbed my hand and pumped. "Boyce assures me that you'll help me bag a trophy-class Dall ram. And he says you may be moving to D.C. soon. You'll have to visit our lab at Georgetown."

Her words hit me like a one-two punch. Bag a Dall ram? Move to Washington, D.C.? Was she out of her mind? I didn't hunt on principle. And moving to D.C.—living anywhere but Alaska, in fact—was out of the question.

I sought out the eyes of my boss, but his gaze dodged away at the approach of a young woman with intricately braided blond hair and a Patagonia pullover in hot pink fleece. She tossed a smile to the small circle around Boyce as she offered him her hand. "Mr. Reade, I'm J. C. Carr, Dr. Cameron's assistant. If you'll point me in the right direction, I'll get him settled and then see to my own luggage."

As they exchanged handshakes, Boyce shot a glance in my direction, a look of stark panic darkening his eyes, but when he managed to speak, the words came out silky smooth. "My apologies, Ms. Carr, but I suppose the initials threw me. I'm afraid I've assigned you and Dr. Cameron to the same tent. We may need some time to sort things out."

Major glitch! My stomach turned another somersault, and for the moment I decided to postpone cross-examining my boss about his assurances that I would be hunting and might be moving. Despite Cameron's sympathetic tut-tuts and J. C. Carr's barely suppressed mirth, Boyce pressed on with his apologies until Margaret Armstrong snagged the arm of a dumpy little man as he passed by, insisting he meet his hosts. For a moment I thought she merely intended to save Boyce from an embarrassing situation, but then I noticed how stiffly the newcomer stood, even as he juggled valise, briefcase and laptop computer, and the mischievous gleam in her dark eyes as she introduced Tom Hart. As he murmured hellos and exchanged brief nods, she delivered her zinger. "In scientific circles, Dr. Hart's known as America's foremost zoologist." Her wide smile had all the sincerity of a coyote's grin. "But those of us working on Gaia know him better as 'Doubting Thomas.'"

For a single excruciating instant, no one said anything. Then I found myself rescued by a ghost from my past. "Lauren?" He towered above me, grayhaired now and softer around the middle, but unmistakably Jack McIntire. Taking my elbow with a surprisingly firm hand, he drew me aside. "I've got trouble, kiddo, and I need your help."

CHAPTER
5

MIDLIFE CRISES LEAVE ME COLD. WHY should hitting middle age be considered the archetypal turning point in life? Why should finally accepting the inevitable sagging of muscle tissue and slowing of synaptic relays be considered some great passage that confers wisdom and maturity? You want maturity, try widowhood at age thirty-five. You want wisdom, try taking that loss and then finding a reason to keep breathing. "Life's a looming battle to be faced and fought," sings Mary Poppins's employer, Mr. Banks, perfectly summarizing the Victorians' Darwinian view of human existence. There's some comfort in that "This-too-shall-pass" equation, even though it means always bracing oneself for the next battle. At least life had some grand meaning for the Victorians. At least their grand crises required solutions a bit more complex than a tummy tuck, a new wife or an inner child.

A child turned out to be the source of Jack McIntire's crisis. Specifically, his eldest, a son who was starting the last year of a lackluster K–12 career in one of the overcrowded teenage warehouses that pass for high schools these days. Since the bus arrived, I'd managed to get our guests settled into their tents. Albert Coppola had graciously returned the mess tent to us, moving his investigation into a park service building on the other side of the campground, and Konstantin Zorich had wandered off in the direction of the lake. Boyce took it upon himself to give the conferees the bad news about Arkady Radishchev and then declared the bar open, agreeing to handle the inevitable questions and exclamations of concern without my assistance. Which left me plenty of time to hear Jack McIntire's tale of woe. When we were in grad school, he'd been the laughing-eyed optimist among a sober crowd of rational determinists. Max always said Jack's joy came from surviving a tour of duty as a U.S. Army officer in Vietnam. Now a bleak heart-clogging anguish smothered all the laughter in my friend's eyes. Children will do that to you.

Jack and I had mixed drinks in the mess tent—a stiff Scotch and soda for him, plain soda for me—and then found a quiet spot on a nearby bench carefully aligned for a head-on Denali view. Jack had spared one glance for the mountain before launching into his sad story. "Tommy's always been a good kid, Lauren. In elementary school, he was a space nut, read everything he could about rockets and even built a couple. Then, in junior high, everything just went to hell."

I fanned a no-see-um away from my ear and tried to hide the uneasiness creeping over me. Not that I didn't want to support my old friend, but I hoped he'd spare me the details. Call it a self-defense mechanism. When Jack mentioned "junior high," a sudden chill lifted the hair on my arms. That's where my Jake was heading in the next few days, and like all parents facing that wrenching transition, I was plagued by doubts and fears. Would the teachers know Jake was one of the good kids if I didn't volunteer in the classroom every week? Could those girls with long legs and real breasts actually be in eighth grade? How had Jake managed to finish elementary school as such a bad speller? And did those other boys, the ones with the sullen eyes and foul mouths, even know how to read?

As if he'd read my mind, Jack's lips twisted into a sneer. "Kids these days can't read, and do you know why? Because there are forty kids in his classroom. And a bunch of 'em are Mexicans who don't speak much English. And another bunch are Vietnamese who don't have much English, either. And the teacher's a nitwit who barely scraped through some moronic state teacher's college." He stared at the mottled bark of a huge spruce, the bitter edge in his voice further shredding my memories of a happier man. "Is it any wonder that Tommy can't get into college?"

I sucked in a sliver of ice and let it melt under my tongue. It looked like I had an example of that new species on my hands—the angry white male. He's all the rage in the media these days, touted as the festering canker of the body politic, an ironic symbol for the last days of the American century. Except he's not always white, he's not always male and he's not always angry. For many members of my generation, scared is more like it. Life wasn't supposed to turn out this way. We were the generation who expected smooth sailing but found ourselves in rough seas tossed by squalls like recession and typhoons like global competition. We never questioned our right to the good life, and now many of us find ourselves watching it slip away. There's not enough money for a second home. There's not enough money for a country-club membership. There's not enough money for a trip to Europe. And just possibly there's not enough money to send Junior to the old alma mater. From white collar to blue collar in one generation—that's what worries all of us, including guys like Jack. But my friend had an ace in the hole—a tenured position on the faculty of one of America's premier public universities. Meaning free tuition. So what was the problem? So, I asked him.

"Getting him in. That's the problem." Jack drained the Scotch from his glass and rattled the leftover ice. "Competition's incredibly tough, even for faculty kids. And I'm out of favor with the administration, to say nothing of politically incorrect." He tossed me a rueful grin. "Candor is definitely not appreciated on campus these days."

I looked at him then, all gray and pudgy and out of his element, dressed in old fatigues and a hooded sweatshirt, the kind of wilderness wear that went passé in the 1970s. And I remembered a night in the lab when I had worked way too late, almost burned out my brain by staring too hard at the wiggling specimens on the slide under my high-powered microscope. Somehow I just couldn't see the features I needed to find. Everything blurred and the lab work had to be done by eight A.M. I'd put it off until the last minute, and now I was up against the wall. Tears of self-pity dripped from my chin when Jack McIntire found me scrunched over that damned microscope. And with all the joy and laughter and love of life that was in him, he made me look again, helped me see for the first time in a very long time the miracles of life that pervade our planet. I had said to him that night in the lab what I repeated this day in the forest. "You're a great teacher, Jack."

He lifted his chin and nodded. "One of the best, kiddo. Which is part of the problem. Great teachers don't make great researchers and vice versa. I made my choice a long time ago, and that was my one big mistake."

"Mistake?" His words drained the warmth from my memory, and I set the glass of icy soda in the dust at my feet. What the world needs now is teachers just like Jack. "How can being a great teacher ever be a mistake?"

"When you can't afford new tires for your car. When your little girl can't have the dress she wants for the prom." He dipped his head and glanced away. "When you raid the youngest's savings account to scrape together the air fare for a conference in Alaska."

"My God, Jack! Every day there's another story about the fat paychecks in academia. Is it just more talk-radio flapdoodle?"

My word choice actually prompted a smile, one that didn't reach his eyes. "The hotshots are very well paid, especially the Nobelists. Which is as it should be. Plus they earn extra pay from the research grants they bring in. And I'm very well paid—by national standards. But try living on sixty-five K a year in the Bay area. Christ, it's all I can do to keep the kids in shoes. Every snotty undergrad has a better car and nicer clothes than I can afford."

"Why don't you move?" My practical self blurted the words before I could cork them. "I mean, is that a possibility?"

"Not for a guy like me." He lifted his shoulders into a shrug and sighed. "Too much tenure for the junior positions. And not enough research or prestige for the senior slots. Too little bang for way too much bucks. Meaning I'm stuck in my rut for the foreseeable future. With three kids coming up, I can't afford any change that's less than an absolutely sure thing."

Stuck. Maybe that's the secret ingredient of the

midlife crisis. By our forties, most of us have labored long enough at our careers to be well and truly sick of the work. As young rebels, we swore to quit any job that got routine, brave words spoken well before the birth of Junior, Princess and The Baby. Now sagging in the harness and endlessly tripping over the same damned stone in our rut, we look up to discover our young beauties blooming with youth and vitality and endless promise. After that discovery, the bravest and the best among us prepare to go the distance, knowing full well that when our race is run, all the youth and vitality and promise of our own lives will be gone. Quiet desperation, Henry David Thoreau termed it from his philosopher's bench beside the shore of Walden Pond. Sitting on a bench beside a wilder shore, I finally understood what he meant.

"How can I help you, Jack?" I leaned toward him until my head touched his soft but sturdy shoulder. "I'll do anything I can."

His arm came around me for one quick squeeze. "No big deal, kiddo. Write a letter to Cal for Tommy."

I had my doubts about how his boy would fare at "Berserkley" and voiced them as I straightened up. "You don't think someplace smaller might be better for your son?"

"What Berkeley has that Tommy needs is me." He rattled the ice in his glass once more and then pitched it at the spruce. "I think it's time this great teacher helped his own kid."

I had to trust Jack's judgment about the needs of his own son but confessed serious doubts about the weight my words would carry with the admissions people. "I'm happy to write a letter, but it's not like I have much visibility, you know. I'm not active with the alumni and, as a field biologist, don't have much influence within the department."

Without warning, he reached over and took my hand, cradling it against his cold palm, still chilled from the icy glass. "They do think well of you, Lauren, and they worshipped Max."

At the mention of his name, tears filled my eyes. Sometimes I almost hated Max for dying. I wouldn't have been nearly so nervous about Jake's junior high debut if his father had been around to keep him centered. Although Max certainly shared every parent's fears, he also exhibited a high degree of confidence in his ability to make sure his children not only survived but also thrived. Hands-on fathering was his name for the kind of labor-intensive parenting that made him a huge presence in his kids' lives. When I took over the job as a solo, I dubbed my effort the grizzly-bear school of mothering. So far so good, as the saying goes, but as Jack McIntire reminded me, these days things can go bad for kids very, very fast.

At the sight of my tears, Jack hauled me into his arms, hugging me against him with surprising strength. "God, he was a good man, Lauren. You must miss him something awful."

For a long moment, I allowed myself the luxury of his embrace. Then I leaned back in his arms, wiped the tears from my cheeks and tried for a smile. "Even after all these months, I still take it one day at a time. And I'm not even in a twelve-step program!"

On that note, we headed back to the mess tent, where the conferees had sorted themselves into smaller groups that buzzed with conversation. Jack made a beeline for the bar while I angled through the tables, intent on buttonholing Boyce, who stood alone near the door that connected with the kitchen tent. He didn't look happy to see me coming but had the good grace not to run.

"Where should we start?" I marched right up to him and squared my shoulders, ready for battle.

"With the trophy-class Dall ram or with the move to D.C.?"

Before answering, he took my elbow, steering me through the steaming kitchen tent and into the fresh air outside. "I'm sorry, Lauren. I'd just started to tell you when Zorich shouted after discovering Radishchev's body." He spread his opened hands, mimicking the ancient way of showing oneself unarmed. "Margaret Armstrong called about it when I was on vacation. She knew we had staff in Alaska and assumed you'd provide guide service. The Washington crew was so dumbfounded by her insensitivity to our mission that they waited for my return. By the time I got back to work, we couldn't afford to offend her and risk scuttling the whole conference, so, reluctantly, I agreed to arrange the hunt. At that point, you weren't even coming to this conference."

He paused, seeming to expect a response, but I remained silent. Let him roast for a few moments. Inside the kitchen tent, the chef and his helpers clattered pans, but the silence outside proved unbearable to Boyce, and he plunged ahead. "When our plans changed, I decided to tell you in person rather than by phone. Quite honestly, I thought I'd have a better chance of talking you into it in person."

Another pause, much shorter, and then Boyce Reade actually scuffed his toe in the dirt at our feet. "I'm terribly sorry, and I hope you'll forgive me. It's a wretched situation, and I accept full responsibility. I should have set things right as soon as I returned from sailing with the children."

The man had taken his kids sailing and asked my forgiveness for his blunder. And if I'd found myself in his position, I probably would have done exactly the same thing. Margaret Armstrong's disapproval would scuttle our Gaia conference. We needed her a lot more than she needed us.

"I'll take the damned woman hunting. But out-of-state hunters are required to have a licensed guide, which means hiring a friend of mine named Travis MacDonald. I know you'll agree." At his eager nod, I relaxed the ramrod posture a bit. "And I'll do my damnedest to talk her out of killing a ram. However, before we get around to forgiving, why don't you tell me about my move to D.C.?"

At my question, Boyce finally looked out across the lake to the wonder that is Denali, his glacier-shawled shoulders now stained here and there with afternoon's purple shadows. "Things are changing in Washington. We may soon have a real fight on our hands."

He looked back to me, eyes clouded with an emotion I couldn't define. "I know you love this great land, Lauren. And I know you'd like to live here always. But saving this place will require great sacrifices of all Americans, including you. To save Alaska, you may have to leave Alaska."

CHAPTER
6

LEAVE ALASKA?

The question haunted the rest of my day, a brooding background refrain to my duties as hostess. Not that any sourdough has passed a year in the Great Land without giving the idea at least some serious thought. On a bleak winter morning, for instance, when the Alaskan has forgotten to plug in the car's engine heater and discovers the subzero temperature drained all the juice from his battery. Or maybe late one midsummer night when the kids can't sleep and keep going strong in the midnight sun. Those who want a Coppertone glow have to leave because even a thousand hours of exposure to that sun won't tan pale skin one shade darker. When a marriage, birth or death forever changes the life of some special person in the Lower 48, Alaskans are just too damned far to be there. And the Great Land's farness and freedom exposes her inhabitants to ghastly accidents that leave empty places at many tables, including mine. For a time after Max's plane disappeared, I hated Alaska, hated the very things that drew him to it—wild rough edges and brutal vigorous energy. But when I considered moving somewhere safer and saner, every other place seemed drab and boring in comparison. Alaska killed the man I loved, and still I couldn't leave. Could the threatened death of Alaska itself persuade me to leave the Great Land?

After a bit of mingling in the bar-cum-mess-tent, I could stand no more. Exchanging names and get-to-know-you trivialities failed to drown that brooding refrain in my mind. I needed either time to think or a major distraction. Preferring the latter option, I headed off toward Wonder Lake in search of Konstantin Zorich, a fellow whose personal and legal troubles would certainly put my worries in perspective.

The late afternoon sun added a ruddy tint to the reflection of serrated granite and glacial ice that decorated the placid water. From the woods near the public campground, a half dozen whooping kids emerged, so I turned toward the far shore. The pungent boggy aroma of the lake perfumed the air. For a quarter mile, a lacework of paths wound among the stunted spruces and leafy alders, evidence of many explorers. About a third of a mile out, the paths had finally converged into one trail, hugging the shore. Most national park visitors rarely stray off the beaten path, and Denali visitors are no exception. What inclination many might have is lost in the face of the grizzly information at park headquarters, for which American taxpayers should be forever grateful. We already spend *beaucoup* bucks pulling stranded climbers off the mountain. Nobody wants rescue parties for lost hikers or search-and-destroy hunts for rogue bears.

I followed the solitary trail farther away from camp, finally spotting a fresh boot track in the dirt and another mashed into a fairly fresh mound of what could have been bear scat. My own fear of the griz inspired me to pick that moment to start whistling, just in case. I'm not sure what inspired me to warble "The Battle Hymn of the Republic," but from around the next bend came an answering whistle—"The 1812 Overture"—and mere seconds later, the man responsible appeared. As he closed the distance between us, Konstantin Zorich waved his hands conductor-style.

"Sorry to disturb your solitude." I didn't want to come off as overly dramatic and lifted my shoulders into a shrug. "Lets the bears know I'm coming."

His eyes blazed with enthusiasm. "You are seeing grizzly bears? Where?"

"Not in the fur." I pointed at the ground. "Just their leavings on the trail."

The light in the Russian's eyes glittered as he halfheartedly nudged the scat with one boot. "This bear is eating berries these days, feeling very well."

I tilted my head and studied him, noting the lines of fatigue etching his face. Obviously, the reality of Arkady Radischev's death had finally deflated the euphoria of last night's star-struck hike to Wonder Lake. How long had it been since he'd slept, anyway? "More importantly, how are *you* feeling?"

He had no answer beyond a quick shrug and the rapid blinking of his eyes. So I just took his arm and nudged him into motion, retracing his own steps down the trail. After a few moments, I asked a simple question. And after a few moments more, he provided a simple answer. And so it went, question and answer, question and answer, until interrogation gave way to conversation.

I began by asking Konstantin Zorich about his childhood, and he told me about growing up in a sterile Soviet-style apartment complex on the outskirts of Moscow, the only child of two high school teachers, both mathematicians. Two rooms, a cubicle kitchen and a bath down the hall—a typical Soviet home, right down to the lumpy couch in the main room that doubled as Konstantin's bed. And outside the typical Soviet landscape—cracked concrete, muddy paths, spindly trees stripped of leaves by the acid rains from a nearby power plant. He lived from summer to summer, throwing himself into his schoolwork from September to May and then escaping from June to August to his grandfather's *dacha* near the Ural Mountains.

"For me, heaven is there." His eyes went dreamy as he stared at the granite peaks above us. "School as well. In summer am I tutored in all that must not be taught in Soviet school. Once Grandfather is famous teacher. Now he has but one pupil. Me."

At a branch in the trail, I took the fork heading for the water. When we reached the edge of the shore, water lapping against the stones near our boot toes, I prompted him again. "He was retired?"

"Nyet."

Hard to imagine that one word could hold so much bitterness. A tingle of unease ran up my spine, and I bent down to search along the shore for something flat and skippable. When I found a likely stone, I straightened and faced him squarely. "What happened?"

"Trofim Lysenko." Zorich followed up the name by spitting into the lake. "A stupid peasant. And his comrade, Stalin." He spit again. "'Man of Steel' is also peasant. For those two, we should crawl back into the caves."

The stone I held bit into my palm as my fingers squeezed into a fist. Boyce Reade had sketched in the outlines of Lysenko's assault on Russian science, but Konstantin Zorich provided the human story in the tale of his grandfather, a brilliant plant geneticist whose career floundered after he publicly defended colleagues working on agricultural problems. In the first decades of the twentieth century, Russian genetics was the envy of the world, an intellectual powerhouse fueled by a Tsarist reform that invested heavily in scientific and technical schools. Unfortunately, the reforms never reached the countryside, where the peasantry remained mired in superstition and ignorance. And so, the great agricultural innovations created by genetics never reached Russia's farms, which languished with inferior seeds, low yields and crude technology. Into the breech stepped Lysenko, a quack breeder who promised to revolutionize Russian agriculture.

"For sweeter apple, water orchard with sugared water. For greater yield, plant winter seed in summer season." Zorich shook his head. "For what you want, wish and it shall be."

I sidearmed the stone across the water, getting only two skips out of the effort. Following my lead, the Russian bent down in search of a skipping stone. "Such fools. All of them fools. And Stalin greatest of all."

I moved off in search of a stone of my own but tossed a question back to him. "Tell me about your grandfather."

He straightened and practiced his throwing motion a few times before finally letting his stone fly. The old man managed to hold on through most of the 1940s but, with the Cold War making lots of people mighty nervous, finally lost his job and retired to his *dacha*. His most brilliant student, Arkady Radishchev, lit out for the East, figuring he wouldn't be bothered as long as he stayed away from Lysenko's agricultural turf. Tundra botany became his specialty.

I scooped up a half dozen likely stones before moving back toward him. "So that's how you met Radishchev? Through your grandfather?"

Zorich paused to inspect the handful of stones that I offered and selected two before continuing. "In time, my grandfather sent me to Arkady in Siberia. In that frozen empty place would I find freedom, he promised."

I tried for a gentle toss and this time was rewarded with four skips that shattered the placid reflection of granite and ice. "And did you find freedom in the Siberian emptiness?"

"Of a kind, yes. Freedom was there, and also my great friend." He flung his stone, and it sank without one skip. "Without him now will Siberia truly be cold and empty."

For a while we concentrated on skipping stones. His sailed far past mine, but my tosses produced far more skips. I showed him my technique—level trajectory about waist-high and a full-arm motion culminating with a flick of the wrist—and then he managed a few skippers amid many sinkers. After I'd taught him all of my best stuff, Zorich let fly his last stone, and the volume of his voice built as he counted every skip. *"Raz, dra, gree, chitiree, pyats, shest, sim, vosem, deyayrits, deyasitis!* Ten!" He grinned broadly and pointed at the string of widening circles that traced his rock's path. "Ten!"

The Russian's shout flushed an osprey from an overhead branch, and the fish hawk loosed her distinctive high-pitched cry as she flew off instead of tucking her wings to dive-bomb into the water in search of prey. What with the skipping stones and the exuberant shout, she'd probably have better luck at the new lake that had formed in a nearby drainage. Zorich watched her flight, a sad smile grooving his face, until the osprey became a pin dot that disappeared against the deep greens of a distant forested ridgeline. "Some days I, too, am wishing to fly away."

I touched his arm. "Today included?"

He shrugged again, this time without needing to blink back tears, and heaved a great sigh. All of a sudden his face looked a hundred years old. "Perhaps, yes, if your police are deciding I killed my great friend."

I took his arm again, drawing Zorich back onto the trail in the direction of camp. If we hurried, he could still catch an hour or two of sleep before dinner. For some reason I felt very protective of the Russian. "Albert Coppola's not a policeman. He's just a park ranger, but tell me what you told him, anyway."

Zorich glanced at me, his eyes clouded by doubt, but he sketched in the content of his statement. After arriving at the Wild America camp at Wonder Lake in the hour before dawn, the Russians had chosen a tent at random and crept inside, intending to sleep a bit before making their presence known. Almost immediately, drowsiness overtook Kontantin, but the excitement of the moment left Arkady Radishchev wired.

"For so many years he is laboring in Siberia, not known and not celebrated, his genius a state secret. And now to be coming here." With his free arm, he swept a half circle that embraced the entire Alaska Range. "To be meeting Thomas B. Hart! To be conferring with James Cameron! Of course, Arkady is not sleeping! Who could be sleeping at such a moment?"

I noticed he didn't mention the honor of meeting Margaret Armstrong. Could the reputed Russian sexism make it impossible to recognize a woman's genius? Before I could ponder that question, Zorich disarmed me with his honesty. "Of course, soon I am sleeping. And when I am awake, tent is empty and Arkady is gone."

The whoop of children's voices somewhere up ahead signaled our nearness to the campground at the head of Wonder Lake, meaning I had to hurry things along if I wanted to hear the whole story before we arrived. "So you went looking for him? And cried out when you found him? And then we came running?"

Zorich nodded firmly in response to each of my questions. "All this I am telling your police."

By now the single trail had given way to the lacework of paths. I dropped his arm as we skirted a low bush cranberry, each taking the opposite path. When we came back together on the other side, I tried—as diplomatically as possible—to reassure him, sounding more than a little bit Pollyannaish as I proclaimed ideals that hardly anyone upholds anymore. "In America people are innocent until proven guilty. I suppose that whole idea may be outside your experience, but for the most part it's true."

He didn't seem convinced, so I plunged on, confident in my own instincts about Zorich's innocence even as I wondered whose name topped Coppola's list of suspects. "I know you didn't kill your friend. And I know you have nothing to worry about from the police."

Another doubtful glance from the Russian brought another assurance from me. "Really."

He stopped suddenly and turned to face me. "And what of you, Lauren Maxwell? The police have the gun. Are you worrying?"

Talk about blowing hot and cold. My innards froze, even as I shook my head. "Coppola's got *my* gun, but it's not *the* gun."

Zorich frowned and tilted his head as he studied my face. "A new police is here, a woman, and he told her. 'I have the gun,' he said. And then he is talking about the wound, and they are sniffing the gun and scratching blood from the metal."

Ice encased my heart, and I squeezed the words out. "What kind of gun?"

Konstantin Zorich put a steadying hand on my shoulder and looked deep into my eyes. "The kind you are bringing to the police. The one he is putting in the little bag."

My gun. Who would Coppola's suspicions focus on now? Me. Next question?

CHAPTER
7

Mᴙ GUN THE MURDER WEAPON?

I'd gone down to the lake in search of distraction but found a waking nightmare instead. A chorus of vicious harpies infiltrated my head, bellowing in unison: *murder weapon, murder weapon, murder weapon!* Albert Coppola believed that my gun killed Arkady Radishchev. Impossible!

Konstantin Zorich kept pace with me as I marched back down the trail at full stomp. The head ranger must be certifiable. My gun the murder weapon? Ridiculous!

At my approach, a red squirrel chattered furiously from his perch in a twisted spruce, but I didn't pause to study the critter. My gun the murder weapon? Nonsense! And that nonsense had to end—starting here, starting now.

After skirting the public campground, I headed straight for the complex of park service buildings that anchored the western end of Denali Park with the Russian still trotting beside me. "You know where he is?" I swept a hand toward the cluster of wooden buildings. "You know which one Coppola's using?"

Zorich pointed to the far end of the complex, indicating a long building that looked like a bunkhouse. "Last building is hers."

Hers? That stilled my marching feet. "Whose?"

Zorich spoke slowly, enunciating each word carefully, making sure I got the message this time. "The woman police I am hearing talk about your gun. Agent Malloy. She is from FBI."

Maybe you had to grow up in the days of J. Edgar Hoover to appreciate the sinister portent in that acronym. Even the mental picture of cross-dressing Hoover's bulldog jaw jutting from the lace collar of some demure little number didn't diminish that instinctive dread. Could be we owe that awe to Efrem Zimbalist, Jr., and the rest of the cast of the 1960s TV show, "The FBI." Didn't they always get their man? Or woman? No matter how it happened, my indoctrination seemed complete. Moisture dampened my palms even as my mouth shriveled with drought. Three little letters—*FBI*—but, oh, what a dire omen for someone whose gun they believed to be a murder weapon!

I drew in a deep breath and let the air leak out slowly, hoping to quiet my thumping heart. Why did they think my gun was the murder weapon? Why hadn't they questioned me? And why was I still standing out in the clear where they might see me?

Just then a young woman in a navy blazer pushed open the screen door of the end bunkhouse, making retreat impossible. No way out but forward, so I advanced straight toward the jaws of hell. Her gaze flicked over Zorich's face before settling on my own, a green-eyed gaze made all the more vivid by the sleek black cap of hair that curved to her chin. She had superior position at the top of the steps, but I had surprise on my side. "Let's see your badge, or was that just TV?"

A smile ghosted across her face as she reached into her blazer and came up with a leather wallet. She flipped it open and offered me her credentials. "Special Agent Malloy. Federal Bureau of Investigation."

I studied the badge. "Efrem Zimbalist, Jr., never did it better. Thanks." Raising my eyes to meet Malloy's, I kept up the attack. "You've got my gun. Now I'm told you believe that my .45 killed Arkady Radishchev. I want to know why. And I also want to know why I wasn't told."

Without waiting for an invitation, I climbed the stairs, yanked open the screen door and moved into the shadowed interior of the bunkhouse, leaving Malloy and Zorich to sort things out for themselves. In one corner of the room, Albert Coppola leaned over a battered wooden desk, moving his pen across a page that held his attention. A matching desk stood empty in the opposite corner, close by a picnic table decorated with a few piles of paper, a neat row of Polaroid photos and a half-dozen zip-lock bags—not including the one containing my Colt. A double row of bunks filled the rest of the cabin, each topped with a thin mattress rolled up and tied with twine. The sweet mustiness of disuse hung in the air.

I stalked over to Coppola's desk. "Thanks for keeping me informed about the status of my gun."

The sharp words brought his head up fast. "Sorry, Lauren, but I'm no longer in charge." He carefully recapped his pen before sliding it back into his chest pocket. "I think she was getting around to you, in any case."

Behind me, the screen door thumped closed, so I hiked a hip on Coppola's desk, ready to return Malloy's greeting. "Indeed, she was. Thanks for stopping by to see us, Mrs. Maxwell."

Zorich hadn't made it inside, which was just as well. I'd asked my questions. Malloy could either answer those or ask some of her own.

"I was just on my way to find you." She shrugged out of her blazer, slung it over the chair at the opposite desk and rolled up her sleeves, then crossed the floor to face me. "I suspect your gun because it's been fired recently, shows a spot of blood on the barrel and the caliber's consistent with Radishchev's wound."

A straight answer, but she'd evaded one of my questions. Without thinking, I crossed my arms and then silently cursed myself for the self-protective body language. After all, I had nothing to hide. To cover my discomfort, I went back on the attack. "Why wasn't I told?"

A flash of something unreadable brightened her eyes for a moment. "I'm not in the habit of sharing suppositions, only facts. That means waiting until it's established that your gun definitely killed Arkady Radishchev." She glanced at Coppola. "And I wasn't aware that Zorich overheard our conversation. I'm sorry you had to hear it from him first."

As graciously as I could, I accepted her apology and asked when the facts about my gun might be established.

"I expect a preliminary finding in twenty-four to thirty-six hours—as soon as the autopsy is complete—if the slug's not too damaged." She leaned against the other corner of Coppola's desk. The tension arcing between us like a short circuit proved too much for the chief ranger. He scooted his chair back a couple of feet, but the FBI agent ignored him. I had her full attention. "Mind if I ask you a few questions about today's events?"

The temptation to request a lawyer almost overpowered me, but in the end I managed to resist the urge. Despite my civics lecture to Zorich, I knew that in practice the presumption of innocence all too often turns out to be empty words. "If he's innocent, why does he need a lawyer," we ask ourselves. "And if she's not guilty, how come the cops arrested her?" In many cases, accepting the constitutional protections, which the nation's founders fought to obtain, leads our fellow citizens to presume guilt. No way I'd risk that with the feds. "Sure thing." I shrugged to hide my helplessness and wound up blurting out a stupid quip. "Fire away!"

Malloy clasped her hands like a prim little miss. "Are you aware that firearms are prohibited within national parks?"

Ouch! First question and already I was in the wrong. "Yes, I'm aware of that."

She raised her eyebrows. "You were aware of the prohibition and still brought a weapon into this park?"

I raised my eyebrows right back at her. "Yes, I did, just like thousands of other tourists each year. The bears at Denali aren't like Yogi and Boo-Boo." I tilted my head, sizing her up, and caught sight of Albert Coppola out of the corner of my eye. His resigned nod heartened me no end. I actually went back on the attack. "Ever been charged by a grizzly, Special Agent Malloy?"

The eyebrows came down into a glower. "No, I have not, but that's beside the point."

"We've already established your point. I was attempting an explanation." I fought to keep the shrill tone out of my voice and showed my harmless intent by spreading my hands. "My question wasn't provocation, merely information. If you'd been charged by a grizzly, you'd understand why I brought a gun to Denali, even though weapons possession inside the park violates federal law."

For a moment, she didn't respond. Then she gave a tiny shrug. "Let's move on. Ranger Coppola tells me you carry your weapon in a holster. Were you wearing it today?"

"Part of the day. Until midmorning, when my boss asked me to put the .45 away. The sight unnerved him." A smile flitted across Malloy's face. "Then I left the holstered gun on the campaign table in my tent until turning the Colt over to Ranger Coppola. If my gun turns out to be the one that killed the Russian, someone must have taken it long enough to do the shooting and then put it back. When I retrieved the automatic for the ranger, it didn't appear to have been moved."

Crossing her arms, Malloy rose from the desk and walked away. Coppola swiveled in his chair, but I only followed her with my eyes. "Did you hear any shots fired in that time?" She spun to face me. "Or at any time since, say, midnight?"

"Nope." I shifted my hips, resettling myself against Coppola's desk. "But I was asleep between midnight and six this morning. I didn't hear anything after I woke up."

"Where was your gun while you slept?"

"Same place—in the holster on the campaign table in my tent." I looked away, trying to visualize the distances in the tent. "Probably about seven feet from my pillow. I'm a pretty heavy sleeper. I suppose someone could have borrowed it during the night."

Malloy raised her eyebrows at that and quickly fired back with another question. "Were you alone in your tent?"

A flash of heat stained my cheeks. "Yes. I was alone in my tent."

"All night?"

I gave her a three count, making no attempt to keep a look of disgust off my face. "Yes. I was alone in my tent all night. From the time I entered—probably a bit before ten P.M.—until the next morning when I left for breakfast—my alarm went off at six A.M.—I was alone in my tent."

She nodded, apparently not too impressed by the precision of my words. "And did you leave the tent for any reason? To use the rest room, maybe, or take a walk by the water?"

I shook my head. "I took a bus straight through from park headquarters, drowsing all the way, and was plenty groggy when I arrived. Boyce Reade showed me to my tent, and I collapsed into my sleeping bag. Except for kicking off my shoes, I didn't even bother to undress."

Malloy crossed to her desk and took a few minutes to jot down some notes on a legal pad. Then, pad in hand, she resumed her questions. "To summarize your statement, you're saying you entered the tent around ten P.M., went straight to sleep, slept until the alarm went off at six A.M. and neither heard gunshots nor left the tent in that eight-hour period?"

"That's right." A wave of relief coursed through me, and I threw her a brief smile. She'd gotten the facts straight, at least. "Like I said, I'm a pretty heavy sleeper."

Malloy cocked her head to one side. "Now tell me about this morning."

I lifted my shoulders into a shrug. "Not much to tell. I met Boyce for breakfast, and then he showed me around camp. We were over at the fire ring when we heard Konstantin shouting." Unbidden, the image rose in my mind of the two Russians locked in their bloody embrace. "When we got to them, it was obvious that Radishchev was dead. Konstantin seemed genuinely shook up."

Malloy made no reply and simply studied my face. The pause drew out into an awkward silence. When I could stand it no longer, I blurted out what appeared to me to be the crux of the issue. "If my gun did kill Arkady Radishchev, someone must have taken it from the desk in my tent, used it and then returned it. I guess that's the most likely scenario."

"Maybe. But there is another possibility. Several really." Malloy hugged her elbows and shifted her weight to one foot. "A lost Russian looking for a place to sleep could have blundered into your tent. Nobody could really blame you for firing. After all, Radishchev spoke no English. And I don't expect you speak Russian. That must have been pretty scary."

Clong! At those calm and reasonable words, my heart seized up. For an unending moment I couldn't breathe. Why hadn't I asked for a lawyer? She actually thought I killed him! I glanced at Coppola, who didn't look surprised by her accusation. Obviously, she'd given her theory a test drive, which really made me mad. "No!" The word burst out like a growl. "That never happened."

She shifted her weight to the other foot. "Maybe you heard something out there. Thought it might be a grizzly. You admitted yourself that's why you brought an illegal firearm into the park. Maybe you decided to seek out the grizzly rather than huddle inside that tent, waiting for the bear to find you."

"No!" I rose from the desk and squared my shoulders, not sparing another glance for the park ranger, concentrating all my energy and attention on the real threat. I couldn't let her finish. She was making this up right before my eyes, creating yet another phony scenario. "That never happened, Malloy. That's pure speculation. Is this how the FBI works a case? Make up a story and see who fits the fantasy?"

For the first time, she truly smiled, a wide grin that lit those eerie green eyes. "Maybe he startled you. Maybe he grabbed you. For all we know, he's a rapist.

Either way, no one could blame you. A woman has a right to defend herself."

I shot a final glance at Coppola, who sat there silently, shaking his head. But at what? Her wild fantasies or my fierce denials? Did it matter? Malloy obviously had him cowed.

The FBI agent had rocked back on her heels, still grinning. For the first time since grade school, I wanted to punch somebody's lights out, hungered to ram my fist right in her flat belly and watch her slump over in agony. Instead, I marched out of that bunkhouse just the way I'd marched in, moving past Malloy without a glance or a word. It looked like I had better get very interested in Arkady Radishchev's death and very fast. All of a sudden, this wasn't about solving a mystery. Now this was about saving my own skin.

CHAPTER
8

SAVING MY OWN SKIN MEANT FINDING out exactly who did kill Arkady Radishchev, and for that task I needed the help of Konstantin Zorich. Since Denali Park lacked the mean urban streets that are the hallmark of America's crisis of random violence, I figured the Russian had been killed for a reason. Finding a motive for the scientist's death might help reveal the identity of his killer. Discovering motive usually took a thorough debriefing of a victim's family and friends, and of that circle only Zorich could be reached.

After marching back to the Wild America camp, stomping all the way to squash the jitters that threatened to unnerve me, I went in search of the Russian. The conferees had assembled in the mess tent for dinner, but I detoured through only long enough to scan for my dark-haired quarry and thread between the tables of our fifty guests. Ignoring hails from Boyce and Lawrence Cameron and the temptation of the delicious scent of prawns simmered in a concoction of white wine and shallots, I exited without a word or a bite or the Russian.

Twilight had fallen, and I hadn't even noticed. The last glimmering streaks of an orange sunset stretched toward the jeweled peaks of the Alaska Range. Deep shadows lurked beyond the circle of tents, but someone had lighted torches to mark the way to the campfire circle where Boyce would lead tonight's after-dinner program. Except for the cook and mess tents, no lights showed inside the camp's tents. No matter. A subtle sense of something drew me toward the tent where I'd spent the afternoon watching Konstantin Zorich absorb the shock of his friend's death.

With both flaps and the mosquito netting rolled back, the tent issued an open invitation, and I entered without asking permission. The Russian lay stretched out on his bunk, one hand cocked behind his head. I sat on the other bunk, at the end nearest his pillow. "You're missing dinner."

"Yes, and a fine one, my nose is telling me. But you, too, are missing this meal."

I lifted my hands and then let them drop back into my lap. "I'm not hungry right now."

Though the dusk had faded, enough light remained for me to make out his frown. "So the woman police is upsetting you. Is she telling you how you killed Arkady this way and that way and also another way?"

The question surprised me, and that must have shown because he rolled onto an elbow and continued. "Malloy said I am killing him because he is great scientist or because he is stealing my discoveries or because Siberia is making me crazy." He pantomimed a spit to show his disgust and shook his head. "Russia, America, it makes no difference, I am thinking. Police is police."

"So she pulled the same routine on you." I leaned

forward, letting my arms dangle between my knees. "Do you think she really suspects you, or does she really suspect me?"

Still on elbow, he shrugged his free shoulder. "Malloy is suspecting all of us until the one is found." The constriction in my chest had eased as I talked with Konstantin Zorich. Thanks to his analysis of Malloy's behavior, I now could breathe without effort. And I could even imagine being hungry again sometime. I smiled at the Russian through the gloom. "Maybe later I'll raid the cook tent. Want me to get some goodies for you, too?"

"For us to be nibbling at the singing at the campfire?" He'd surprised me again and flashed a quick grin at my confusion. "Is not why Americans are having fires? For singing like Roy Rogers and Hopalong Cassidy?"

Talk about a blast from the past! I grinned back at him. "Where did you learn about Roy Rogers and Hopalong Cassidy?"

"In my boyhood, from your television. My uncle is high party official, and his children are seeing much American television." He gave a slight shrug. "When I am visiting cousins, I also am seeing your cowboys."

I returned the shrug. "I don't feel much like singing tonight."

He flopped back on his bunk. "Nor do I."

On impulse, I reached over and laid my hand on his arm. "What would you like to do tonight? Sleep? Mourn? Be left alone?"

His free hand came up to cover mine, and he rolled his head until I could see his eyes by the starlight leaking into the tent. "Tonight I would like to walk with beauty under the moon and stars." A faint squeeze of my hand. "Will you walk with me, beauty?"

This was saving my skin on a whole new level. I

wanted to look away but couldn't move my eyes. I wanted to pull back my hand but couldn't find the strength. Since Max died, I'd avoided the eyes of many men, pretending not to see their invitation, and ignored their special touches, pretending not to feel their flirtation. Before I met Max, I believed that the world contained many men who could be my love. But after I fell for him, I knew that while there could be many men *in* my life, Max would be the love *of* my life. And so, like savoring the last drop of fine cognac as long as it lingers on your tongue, I'd spent the years since his death savoring the afterglow of my life's great love. Although I'd accepted the idea that the time must soon come for me to start saying goodbye to Max, I couldn't seem to begin. But now I'd actually reached out to another man, one who'd been as grievously wounded by losing his great friend as I had been by losing Max. Already a twinge of guilt nettled me. Not for the first time, I wondered if those sappy songs had it right after all. Maybe giving *was* the way to begin healing.

I let my fingers tighten, just barely, around the Russian's arm. "Yes, I'll walk with you under the moon and stars."

Across the camp, the screen door of the mess tent opened, silhouetting the familiar perfect posture of Boyce Reade in the square of light that streamed out. He'd be looking for me, of course, and although the fraidy-cat part of me wanted desperately to be found, the bolder, risk-taking part of me urged immediate escape. After passing on a hurried game plan to Zorich, I sidled out of his tent and ducked around the back, heading for the cook tent to pick up a grubstake for our outing.

As planned, we met a few minutes later at the shuttle stop, next to an idling yellow school bus empty of passengers and under the command of one of the long-haired college types who spend their summers working in our national parks. The driver studied us through the fly-specked windshield as I transferred the wine, bread, cheese and fruit I'd lifted from the cook tent into the Russian's battered rucksack. All the while, I endeavored to explain to Zorich why catching a ride to the point down the road that curved closest to the Muldrow Glacier was preferable to setting off cross-country. "I have this thing about bears. We'd have to skirt the McKinley River all the way." I settled the last of the fruit into the bag and, after cinching it closed, hoisted it toward my companion standing above me. "A narrow gravel bar is not where you want to meet a griz. Trust me on that."

He slung the rucksack over one shoulder and offered me his hand, gently lifting me to my feet. "For bears you are carrying weapon?"

"Yeah, but since the feds confiscated my gun, I'd just as soon hitch a ride over the riskiest ground."

It turned out that climbing onto that bus eased my worries in more than one way. The driver nodded to me as we came through the folding doors. "Hello, again." And then he grinned at Konstantin. "Hey, the Russian doc! Welcome aboard. You made it—Eielson to Wonder Lake in one night, but this evening you're riding."

So Konstantin Zorich *had* walked in from the visitor's center. The confirmation warmed me. My instinct and the man had both proved to be true. Which is comforting knowledge when heading off on a moonlit stroll through a six-million-acre wilderness with a complete stranger.

The last streaks of day had darkened to full night when we started for the glacier, a river of ice flowing north that comes within a few miles of the park road. A thick dusting of stars brightened the subarctic sky, and somewhere beyond the peaks of the Alaska

Range, the moon began her rise, embracing the mountains' shoulders in an eerie glow. Within a few minutes, our eyes adjusted to the darkness, and between the moonlight and starlight, we had no problem with navigation or night vision. Gnarled black spruce dotted the low boggy spots of meadow, and thickets of dwarf birch marked the higher ground. The muddy toe of the Muldrow melts into a glacial river, a frigid and silty bath that can't be avoided.

Zorich scouted the bank for a good crossing spot but soon gave up. We stripped off our boots and socks, rolled up our pant legs and braved the icy river. After the first stinging shock, my feet went numb. And dead. Staying upright proved to be the greatest challenge. The Russian made it home free, but I stumbled, wetting myself to the hips. With the temperature of the night air dipping toward forty degrees, frozen feet and wet clothes could mean big trouble. True Siberian that he was, Zorich knew this and immediately gathered driftwood from the gravel bank. I dug a tube of fire ribbon out of my wet pants and we soon had a small fire going. Konstantin crouched beside me, warming his toes for a minute, and then pulled the jug of wine from his rucksack. "Is time for meal."

I leaned closer to the fire, arching my feet. "That's not food."

"Wine is mistake?" He threw me a quick grin. "Or perhaps weapon for bears?"

I grinned back at him. "For the Russian bear. To help the stars and moon shine brightly."

He pulled the cork and lifted the bottle in my direction in a toast. "Ah, beauty, you are outshining everything above."

I accepted the bottle and swallowed a mouthful of mellow red wine. "Say that in Russian, will you?"

In mock passion, he placed a fisted hand over his heart. *"Krasavista, ty zatmevaesh vse na nebe."*

I handed back the wine. "Lovely words in either language."

A jug of wine, a loaf of bread, a wedge of cheese, a half-dozen oranges and a killing to solve. Mixed bag for a moonlit picnic, but we enjoyed it. Konstantin made no pretense of looking away when I shrugged out of my jeans to dry them more easily, and the glow in his green eyes flared higher than the fire. On some fundamental level, Russians aren't very subtle. Consider the exquisite music of Tchaikovsky. However soaring, Mozart's got him beat for complexity. And for all the literary fireworks of Fyodor Dostoyevsky's prose, his finest works never approached Joyce's breathtaking best. Russians are as blunt and clear as the vodka they favor. And just as vivid. In contrast with the smooth moves of our American pseudo-sophisticates, I found Zorich's frank appraisal and lusty vitality incredibly appealing. Which was not the point of this outing. Not the *entire* point, anyway.

While I dug the food out of the backpack, the Russian dug a fresh handkerchief out of his corduroys and spread it on the stones. At the sight of the neat pattern of creases in that makeshift platter, the thought that I had had earlier occurred to me again, and I spoke out loud. "Are you married?"

The dancing light of the fire flickered across his face as he broke off a piece of French bread. "Once I am married, but not now. She, Tatiana, is dead."

Another wound. "I was married, too. And my husband, Max, is also dead." I met his eyes across the flames. "What happened to Tatiana?"

For a second his glance followed a burst of sparks that spewed up. "Of course, you are hearing of Chernobyl?"

Despite the warmth of the fire, the name chilled me. When I finally nodded, Zorich picked up a twig and poked it into the fire. "Then I am working at university in Kiev, and Tatiana is at nuclear plant. After accident they are needing engineer. But who is going—Boris, Mikhail or Tatiana?"

The tip of the twig caught fire, and he drew it out of the flames to study. "Is job for Boris—a man with two tiny babies? Or is job for Mikhail—only son of very poor, very old parents? Or is job for Tatiana—an orphan, no children. For her only there is Konstantin, who is young and strong and healthy. And so she is going."

What can you say at a moment like that? I did the best I could. "She must have been very brave."

The tears in his eyes glittered in the firelight. "Yes, very brave. She goes to Chernobyl a young woman with hair dark like yours. When she is coming home, now is her hair gray. And soon is her hair gone."

The flame inched down the burning twig, leaving a curling tube of ash that finally broke off and drifted to the ground. "But still she is brave. She is coming to America, to Seattle, and doctors are transplanting the marrow of her bones. For many weeks she is very brave and very ill. Then she is dead and must be brave no longer."

When the flame on the burning twig had burned almost to his fingertips, he tossed it back into the fire and looked across the flames, his eyes as cold and empty as the winter skies of the endless Siberian tundra. "And one day I, too, will be going to Seattle and bringing some wildflowers for the grave of my brave Tatiana."

COLD AND EMPTY—THAT'S HOW I EX-
pected to find my tent when we returned to the camp
at Wonder Lake in the hour just before dawn. A
clatter of pans and the glow of light inside the kitchen
tent suggested the possibility of coffee, but neither
Konstantin Zorich nor I needed the buzz. We'd
explored the Muldrow Glacier by moonlight, wandering from the earth-covered toe across the bare ice
until stopped by the first yawning crevasse. On the
way back he'd set a wicked pace, striding through the
darkness with no sign of fatigue on his second sleep-
less night. Just when my energy seriously started to
flag, a second wind kicked in, and by the time we said
good night on the outskirts of camp, every inch of me
glowed, renewed and reborn. Who needed coffee?
Who needed sleep? The questions spilled out of me as
I brushed aside the mosquito netting and entered my
tent, intending to flop on my cot to see if my lighter-
than-air body would actually float.

"I needed sleep, but since you've stolen that from

me, I'll take the coffee instead." Margaret Armstrong raised her gray head from the plump pillow adorning *my* cot. "Cream, no sugar."

I stopped so suddenly that I teetered for a moment, swaying forward and back, as I quickly surveyed my . . . our tent, slowly panning the interior with the beam from my flashlight. She'd stacked my camera, Discman and makeup kit along one edge of the campaign table and placed her laptop computer front and center, along with a neat rank of boxes of microscopic and photographic slides. She'd unrolled my sleeping bag on the opposite bunk, topped it with my pillow and slid my canvas suitcase underneath. A few hangers of her clothes had joined mine on the pole I'd rigged over the foot of the empty . . . my cot. The paperback I'd hoped would lull me to sleep lay spread-eagled on the wooden floor, within reach of Margaret Armstrong's hands. At least she hadn't used my place mark. But she had added a homey touch in the mineral-water bottle holding a bouquet of elkslip and blue monkshood.

I stepped over the book and sat on the edge of my new cot. "I see you've made yourself comfortable."

For the briefest instant, her eyes narrowed, reminding me of an animal ready to pounce. Then she levered herself up, relying almost entirely on her left arm. "I've got a bum shoulder on the right and have to sleep on my left side. I changed bunks so I wouldn't be facing the wall. Have a touch of claustrophobia, too. Do you mind?"

"Not at all." I reached down to unlace my boots. "I'll get that coffee as soon as I change shoes. Didn't you have a tent to yourself?"

She rearranged the sleeping bag around her hips. "I certainly did. However, the confusion about J.C.'s name meant somebody had to share. And she snores.

I learned that the hard way. Boyce assures me that you don't."

Margaret Armstrong eyed me with a sidelong glance, no doubt wondering how my boss had learned of my sleeping habits. Before I could explain the finer points of wilderness camping, she continued. "I suppose Lawrence or somebody could have shared with the other Russian, but under the circumstances, nobody wanted to."

My pulse quickened at the mention of "circumstances," and a spurt of anger gave me fumble-fingers. Forgetting about her curiosity, remembering instead the Russian's heartbreaking stories, I tried to keep my voice steady. "You think Konstantin Zorich killed Radishchev?"

She closed her eyes and massaged her right shoulder. "It's a possibility, but I doubt it." Opening her eyes only to meet my glare, she caught my drift. "The circumstance I meant to suggest is great grief. Boyce Reade told me that the other Russian was quite torn up by it all. No one wanted to intrude."

No one except me. But Zorich didn't seem to mind. I stripped off my double layer of socks—wool and slick—and then snagged a pair of Teva sandals from the bag under my cot. "Cream, no sugar. Would like some pastry if they have it?"

Margaret Armstrong tousled her cropped hair with both hands. "Pastry, fruit—anything they've got! I'm simply famished." She poked her nose close to the net window beside her bed. "Must be all this wonderful brisk air."

I swung by Boyce's tent on the way to the kitchen, expecting a chill blast for abandoning him the night before, but I found only solicitude and understanding. When I outlined Special Agent Malloy's loonytune allegations, he sputtered. And when I described my moonlit hike with Konstantin Zorich, he suggested I sleep till lunch and then rejoin the conferees for the afternoon session. Taking him at his word, I returned to my own tent, carrying a tray loaded with coffee, Danish pastry and a blueberry-sprinkled fruit salad for one and then climbed into my down sleeping bag. Before Margaret Armstrong had finished her breakfast, I'd slipped into a heavy dreamless sleep.

Lunch was long over by the time I crawled out of my cozy nest to find a new tray of food on the campaign table. I poured a glass of the bottled iced tea and swept the napkin from a plate containing an assortment of cheese, crudités, fruit and bread. Between bites, I scrubbed the sleep from my face with a moist towelette and changed into fresh clothes. The warm breeze slithering between the bedside windows promised shorts weather, but I knotted a fleece pullover around my shoulders just in case, then left my tent to search for the scientists.

I found most of our fifty guests perched on the stump stools ringing the campfire pit. The morning had been given over to welcomes and an overview of the Gaia theory from Lawrence Cameron. Two decades earlier, he'd begun to wonder why Earth, the only planet in the solar system to contain life, was also the only planet to have an atmosphere made up of highly reactive gases. Remember high school chemistry, with all those elements that flirtatiously combined and recombined, sharing or swapping electrons, until everything sort of stabilized and reached equilibrium? That drive for equilibrium is the basic tendency of all systems and, on all the other planets, left stable, inactive atmospheres that would be poisonous to the oxygen-breathing life forms on Earth. But although oxygen is just about the flirtiest gas around, always eager to swap or share an electron, Earth's atmosphere has contained twenty-one percent oxygen for hundreds of millions of years and has never come close to equilibrium. How come? Cameron answered that all the Earth's life forms add enough new stuff to the atmospheric mix each day to keep the chemistry from reaching a poisonous equilibrium. In other words, Cameron said, all the individual living organisms acting together make sure that the superorganism—a living Earth known as Gaia—survives.

The thinker behind that theory now sat silently at the head of the campfire circle, listening intently to zoologist Thomas Hart, a man most people in the know identified as the archenemy of Cameron's evolving worldview. On one side of Cameron, Konstantin Zorich sat stiffly erect, a thunderous glower darkening his face, and on the other J. C. Carr took notes on a pad propped against an upraised knee. Across the dead campfire, Margaret Armstrong fidgeted with the hem of her khaki shorts and shot stiletto glances at the fellow who had the floor. I exchanged a quick nod with my boss as I slipped onto the empty stump beside Jack McIntire.

"But, in the end, my rejection of this hypothesis comes on fundamental, even childlike, grounds." Hart ran an idle hand through his dark but thinning hair. A smirk grooved his chubby cheeks as he paused, drawing out the moment, heightening the tension. "If Dr. Cameron is correct and all living things cooperate to regulate the environmental conditions on this planet, I'd like to know where, when and how often this regulatory body meets?" Another pause, just long enough for him to raise his eyebrows as he scanned the circle. "Maybe they can figure out a way to balance the federal budget."

Beside me, Jack McIntire erupted in rumbling

chuckles. A bark of laughter escaped J. C. Carr, drawing a stern glance from Margaret Armstrong, while Konstantin Zorich actually clenched his fists and started to rise. Lawrence Cameron restrained him with a quick hand and deftly redirected the group's attention. "Childlike, indeed. These days few of our colleagues in science value the kind of elegant simplicity that's understandable even to a child." He tilted his head as if considering the small man before him. "And yet the fundamental laws of science are easily grasped by children. Gaia included."

As if on cue, J. C. Carr laid aside her notebook and rose to her feet. "I've got a terrific example! I was just a little girl when man landed on the moon, but my dad had been showing me planets for ages. He's an amateur sky watcher." She shoved her hands into the front pockets of her twill shorts and circled the cold ashes of the campfire. "Mars, Jupiter, Saturn, Venus—I knew them all. Then one day he showed me a photograph of the Earth that had been taken on one of the Apollo missions."

She stopped pacing, and her eyes went dreamy. "I knew all the other planets, but it was my first view of the whole Earth, all blue and green and swirled with clouds. 'It's alive,' I said. Seen from space, the Earth is obviously one living entity, as any child can tell you."

Thinking of the photograph of Earth tacked on the ceiling above Jake's bed, I tilted my head toward Jack McIntire. "That's the way my kids see it."

He greeted that observation with a nod. "Mine, too."

At that moment, Konstantin Zorich jumped to his feet, capturing my full attention. "Is life changing the Earth? Am I breathing?" He breathed in, his hands fanning the air toward his face. "Oxygen in." He exhaled, hands now fanning the air away from his face. "Carbon dioxide out. I am making change to atmosphere. And also you, and also you, and also you." He jabbed a finger at three climatologists from Southern California. "You are breathing, too. So many breathings, so many people—soon will we be poisoned!"

The Russian flung his arms overhead, waving at the trees which surrounded us. "And so are coming the plants to breathe in the poison we are breathing out." He fanned the air in the direction of a venerable white spruce. "Carbon dioxide in." He reversed his motion, fanning the air away from the tree. "Oxygen out."

Konstantin dropped his hands to his sides. "Animals are changing the Earth, and plants are changing the Earth. But all changes are balancing." He strode forward until he loomed over Thomas Hart, who had taken a seat near Boyce Reade. "Balance is where we are seeing Gaia."

The squat neo-Darwinist glanced around the circle and then went for the cheap shot. "Gee, I haven't felt so enlightened since Mrs. Durante's science class in sixth grade."

A momentary confusion clouded the Russian's eyes, but he held his ground until Jack McIntire took up the cause. "Judging by that remark, Dr. Hart, you still belong in the sixth grade." Jack turned his attention to the rest of the group. "Let's hear some other evidence for Gaia that would impress even a child."

Across the fire circle, a young geologist from New Jersey cleared his throat. "What about limestone deposits?"

With all eyes now upon him, the young man blushed but managed to continue. "I took my children to the shore a few weeks ago, and we found a chunk of eroded limestone with fossils visible. They spent all day collecting shells and bits of shells, and then lugged the bucket home. When my wife asked what they planned to do with the shells, they had quick answer." For the first time, he smiled. "'Make rocks,' they said."

"Hah!" Margaret Armstrong took her turn as the center of attention. "As those children could see, our planet literally has been built by the ancestors of all living things, most so tiny that humans didn't know of their existence until a century ago."

She leaned down, scooped up a handful of soil and held out her hand. "There is ten times more life in this handful of dust than the sum of all warmblooded animals in this vast park."

From his stump next to my boss, Thomas Hart threw up his hands. "Here it comes, folks—Margaret and her bacteria."

"Laugh if you will, Doubting Thomas, but the science is indisputable." With seeming reluctance, Margaret Armstrong let the soil sift through her fingers and drift silently toward her feet. "The planet has been so shaped by life as to have achieved life of a kind. That living dance of the Earth and her biota is what Lawrence Cameron calls Gaia. But call it what you will, Gaia is real, Gaia is ancient and Gaia is the reason why this planet, alone among the bodies of this solar system, contains life."

For a second, no one spoke. Then Lawrence Cameron rose to his feet, clapping. "Brava, my dear Margaret. Brava yet again!"

The circle of scientists quickly divided into two circles, a large one surrounding Margaret Armstrong that included Lawrence Cameron, J. C. Carr, Konstantin Zorich and Boyce Reade, and a small circle that surrounded Doubting Thomas. Only Jack McIntire and I stood apart, still hovering before our stools.

He turned toward me with a crooked grin. "In the end, Lauren, does any of it really make a difference? No matter who's right, that doesn't change the fact that one day we'll all be extinct. That's the great lesson in life, my friend. In the end, everything goes to shit."

CHAPTER 10

THE APPROACH OF THOMAS HART
swept Jack McIntire's bleak prognosis from my mind.
Doubting Thomas sauntered across the fire circle,
kicking up ashes and cinders with hiking boots so
lacking in dust or creases that they'd probably been
bought especially for this trip. Which also explained
his scuffing through the fire pit—a little grit and grime
on a boot shows you've really been somewhere.

Hart paused for a second to trade words with Boyce
Reade before homing in on me. I used the moment to
gird for battle. I've never liked people who get their
laughs at the expense of others. And I despise ad
hominem attacks in scientific debate, especially when
the targeted scientist turned out to be a Russian of
whom I'd been growing very fond. However, Hart's
opening move totally disarmed me. "Your boss says I
can tag along on your outing this afternoon. Do you
mind?"

Outing? What outing? With both Hart and Zorich
on the trail, my hike to the new lake could turn into a

warpath, forcing me to play peacemaker. Damn that Boyce! Pretty soon I'd have to brain him one. Since we'd closed the gap between D.C. and Alaska, our working relationship had gone to hell in a hurry. One of the things I liked about my job was answering to no one, except by long distance. Now I'd discovered that one of the things Boyce liked about his job was bossing everybody around.

A 360-degree scan of the sky showed no weather moving in, so I flashed the zoologist my most winning smile. "You're welcome to come." Then I turned my attention to Hart's footwear. "Those look like new boots. Did you remember to wear a second pair of socks, preferably slick ones, next to your feet?"

A sudden flush stained his round face. "Slick socks?"

After making a mental note to bring moleskin for blisters, I explained the physics of hiking and how the two pairs of socks rub against each other instead of chafing the foot. He thanked me for the tip and promised to be outside the mess tent in a quarter of an hour. In the next few minutes, I passed on similar advice and instructions to all the conferees who showed an interest in the hike to Denali Park's newest lake. And I managed to remain civil to bossy Boyce, thanking him for letting me sleep in and reminding him that my pal, Travis MacDonald, would be flying in the next day to help guide Margaret Armstrong to her trophy Dall ram, among other things. I even invited him along on our jaunt, but he begged off, claiming a ton of paperwork demanded his attention. That left us as a party of seven—Lawrence Cameron, Margaret Armstrong, J. C. Carr, Jack McIntire, Konstantin Zorich, Thomas Hart and me.

I swung by my tent to grab the moleskin, a compass and a topographical map and then to the mess tent to provision two rucksacks with hard candy, oranges, granola bars and plenty of water. Not that I expected to be gone very long. One of Albert Coppola's summer rangers had given Boyce precise instructions for locating the unmapped lake, measuring the distance from a starting point just down the road as two miles. I estimated we could make even a five-mile round trip in two hours and have a good fifteen minutes to ooh and ahh over the newborn lake. But wilderness travel requires planning for the unexpected, so I included plenty of provisions, just in case.

Within minutes of leaving camp, my crew had sorted themselves based on fitness, stringing out along the gravel road overlooking the plain of the McKinley River. Not surprisingly, after promising to wait near the bridge that spanned what was left of the creek-cum-lake, J. C. Carr took the lead, setting an ambitious pace with her springing, loose-limbed gait. Konstantin and I followed with matching strides that testified to the hours we'd walked together early that morning. Just in back of us came Margaret Armstrong and Lawrence Cameron, longtime colleagues who also walked together with a practiced ease. Chugging along behind like twin cabooses, Jack McIntire and Thomas Hart paid the price of a sedentary middle age. Or perhaps the stunning view of the Wickersham Wall rising above the autumn plain had slowed them. But, they didn't seem to be arguing—at least not from a distance.

The granite face of the wall drew all eyes, and from Lawrence Cameron came another rhapsody on the subject of Gaia. Although I couldn't hear every word, I caught the gist from the vivid play of emotions—excitement, curiosity, awe—that swept through his voice. Around the next bend, J. C. Carr had stopped by the bridge. While we waited for the cabooses to catch up, I peeled an orange, offering the first section to Lawrence Cameron. A fellow with his appreciation for the Wickersham Wall deserved no less.

For her part, Margaret Armstrong thought the man deserved more, far more respect than he'd been shown by Doubting Thomas at the fire circle, and almost an hour later, she still fumed. "He's an impertinent ass, Cameron, and don't you dare defend him!"

As she glared down the road in the direction of Thomas Hart, Cameron gently patted her arm. "I wouldn't dream of it, my dear Margaret. But surely you see how frightened he is? How confused? With our emphasis on a simplicity that can be grasped by a child, we've called into question the basic assumptions of Big Science. The poor chap's terrified!"

"Big Science?" The Russian tossed in the question. "What is 'Big Science?'"

"Oftentimes folly, my friend." Cameron shook his head at my offer of another section of orange. "An overreliance on technology and models are the hallmarks of 'Big Science.'"

As I passed around the sections of a second orange, he warmed to his subject. "My favorite example comes from Britain's James Lovelock and concerns the ozone hole. By the 1970s, technology allowed us to make very intricate studies of the stratosphere, feeding new data from satellites, weather balloons and flying craft into sophisticated computers."

A stray breeze rustled the young tamaracks beside the road, loosing a cloud of yellowing needles that perfumed the air. Cameron inhaled the zest and smiled. "But the scientists in charge decided they already knew enough about our atmosphere to make predictions and create a model. So they programmed the computer to ignore information that differed from what they expected to find, and therefore ignored the diminishing ozone. As Lovelock pointed out, the data about the ozone hole existed for years, but 'Big Science' didn't care about the facts. Two chaps with antique instruments made the key observations. In person."

I snuck a glance at Zorich, guessing I'd find a small smile of satisfaction at learning that Western science had blockheads of its own who resembled Trofim Lysenko. Just as I'd suspected, his lips curled with private pleasure, which gratified me to no end. My attraction to him hadn't reached the bells and whistles stage yet, but my gut warned me it might. Maybe he was a bit like Officer Chekov from the original "Star Trek," transparently earnest and somehow safe. But how tiring I found the two predominant strains of Alaskan manhood: the Anchorage yuppie with his blasé sophistication or the bush survivalist with his he-man misogyny. What did I like about this Russian? His joy for life. His delight in science. His enthusiasm for work. His admiration of me. I'd seen more than my share of available guys whose worldview consisted of starring in the movie of their own lives. Konstantin Zorich struck me as the genuine article—a real man—and a pretty hard one to resist. All day I'd been debating whether to even try.

When Jack McIntire and Thomas Hart finally joined us, I ignored J. C. Carr's obvious impatience and insisted on a five-minute rest, making sure each of our stragglers ate half an orange and swallowed plenty of water. The unaccustomed exertion had reddened the cheeks of both Jack and Thomas, but their breathing didn't seem particularly labored, and a quick check of the map showed that we wouldn't have to gain all that much elevation to view the lake. With J.C. at my elbow, I indicated our route across the wavy blue lines of the topo map, tracing a series of switchbacks that led to the promontory marked with the ranger's *X*.

She rocked back on her heels. "Why don't we just follow the creek bed?"

"Couple of reasons." I carefully folded the map, making sure to leave our section in view. "As a path, the creek's too muddy and rocky for comfort. And not too far in from this road we'd enter a gorge of sorts, one that won't provide much of a view. Plus we'd be trapped if the debris dam were to rupture."

The best hikes in Alaska tend to be pretty vertical and this one proved no exception. Just back from the road, the ground began to rise, and soon I turned my back on the creek, angling across the slope in a gradual ascent. In general, terrain offers three kinds of climbing: ladder, staircase or ramp. The sheer terrain that mimics a ladder's climb daunts even the experienced hiker, but novices often figure ground as steep as a staircase makes up with speed what was lost to exhaustion. When Max and I first took our kids hiking, back when Jessie still rode on her daddy's shoulders, I had charge of keeping our billy goat, Jake, from scampering straight up the mountain. My gigawatt kid might be one of the few on the planet who could manage that kind of terrain, but, eventually, after many hands-and-knees scrambles, I persuaded him that not everyone shared his Iron Man endurance. Fortunately, of my Denali crew, only J. C. Carr looked tempted by the steeper route and in time she, too, learned the wisdom of the ramp. Think vertical gain. My topo map indicated we'd need to gain 250 feet in elevation to reach the promontory over the newborn lake. Doesn't sound like much until translated into staircases in ten-foot increments. By that equation, the necessary elevation gain would equal twenty-five flights of stairs. Try that climb sometime. Those who do soon understand the attraction of long gradual switchbacks which mimic a ramp.

The ramp of a trail we followed threaded through

white spruce, aspen and tamarack, all plentiful species in the stunted northern woods that the Russians call the *taiga.* Our feet crunched through mats of fallen leaves and needles, spicing the warm air. The understory blazed with autumn colors—crimson, amber, yellow—as shrubs and lichens prepared for the park's other season. Little fruit remained on the crowberry and cranberry, and the occasional wild rose showed only rosehips. The sunlight fell through the canopy of larger trees in golden streams, spotlighting random patches of the forest floor, and the number of insects swimming in those beams of light seemed far fewer than just the day before.

After our next rest break, Konstantin dropped back to walk with Lawrence Cameron and Margaret Armstrong, who turned out to be natural food nuts in search of wild edibles. As we had rested in a small clearing, Cameron smiled when he spotted a spiked plant topped by a cluster of green-and-white flowers. *"Zigadenus elegans*—the Death Camas."

Margaret Armstrong had not been amused. "Don't touch it, Cameron. If you forget to wash your hands, you might get sick!"

"Nonsense, my dear. You have to eat the plant, not just touch it." He'd tossed her a reassuring smile, but I was glad to have the Russian botanist overseeing their selection of wilderness munchies.

As we started off again, I drew J. C. Carr into conversation, hoping to slow the young graduate assistant's ambitious pace. "Sharing that story you told at the campfire circle took some courage. Not all scientists value the insights of children."

She gave me a smile as bright as the warm autumn sunshine. "Thank you, Lauren. I'm afraid I needed that. Unfortunately, Dr. Armstrong doesn't share your opinion." She blinked a couple of times. " 'Soft-headed' is the term she used."

I forced my voice down a few octaves. " 'Emotions have no place in science.' " J. C. Carr's smile widened into a grin, spurring me to more mimicry. " 'Death to wonder! Down with awe!' First thing I noticed under a microscope was how pretty all those little bugs were."

A rich laugh escaped her. "Same with me. The wonder is what sucks you into science, but as soon as you're hooked, they want you to turn into a robot." She shook her head. "Now I worry that I've made a big mistake. Dr. Cameron's great, but all the rest are so damned bloodless. Maybe I should just take a teaching credential and get it over with."

I swatted aside an overhanging branch. Up ahead, the forest brightened. Meaning we were getting close to the edge of the gorge. "How good are you?"

The question surprised her, and she took a while to answer. When she did, her eyes glowed with a new light. "I'm very good."

"Then don't let them chase you away." As we approached the creek's gorge, I slowed my pace, looking beyond her shoulder to judge the nearness of our companions. "Bloodless science has turned people off, and now we're facing global problems that only science can solve. More than ever before, we need scientists who lead with their hearts."

I waited for the others, but J.C. dodged through the fringe of trees that edged the steep gorge until she found the small clearing the ranger had X'ed on my map. She didn't speak when we came up beside her. None of us did. Instead we crept closer and closer until all seven of us stood shoulder to shoulder at the edge.

The earth fell away before us, the steep ravine a testament to the sculpting power of water running free. But now the water far below had been captured, dammed by an enormous slide of earth and rock. A shimmering lake filled the gorge, twisted, narrow and extending far into the foothills. Outcroppings of rock and gnarled tangles of shrubbery adorned the eroded bank below us while the cliff across the lake bore the raw scar left by the dam torn from its flanks. The violent roar of the slide had given way to the placid silence of the lake.

At my elbow, Lawrence Cameron finally broke our silence. "Caused by a small earthquake, perhaps?"

"Could be." I pointed to a dark patch on the opposite wall, a telltale trace of an ice wedge. "See that ice across the way? This is permafrost country. Rain and snow melt and saturate the surface, leaving no place for the water to go but creeks and rivers. High runoff sometimes means massive erosion."

Everyone needed help finding the wedge of ice and they clumped around me, huddling elbow to elbow and knee to knee, all trying to follow the imaginary line that led from my pointing finger to the dark patch of ice on the opposite cliff, all seven of us straining forward to see that example of one storied feature of the Great Land. Then, in the space of a heartbeat, J.C. stumbled and somersaulted off the edge of the cliff, free-falling toward the shimmering lake.

Oh, SHIT!"

I recognized the words that broke the forest silence but not the sound of my own voice, harsh and hollow in my ears. Beyond a gasp and a skitter of pebbles when she went over the edge, J. C. Carr fell without words and without sound. And before I'd even completed my second hoarse syllable, Konstantin Zorich followed her, bounding over the precipice and sliding out of view.

"Shit, shit, shit!" I flung my arms wide like the crosswalk attendant at Jessie's elementary school, determined to keep the rest of my crew from vanishing before my eyes. "Move back! Everybody move back from the edge!"

When the pressure against my arms eased, I spun on my heel and took in the scene with a glance. Margaret Armstrong covered her mouth with both trembling hands as she stepped back from the gorge. A red-faced Jack McIntire flung an arm around a sapling to steady himself while Thomas Hart, eyes wide and popping, opened and closed his mouth like a guppy. Only Lawrence Cameron held his ground, face drained of all color and eyes bleak with horror.

I slung the rucksack off my back, sank to my knees and dug around inside. "I want you to stay right here and stay back from that edge." After pulling out two water bottles, I fished around for fruit and granola bars, finding a handful of each. "I'm going to go down to her and send Konstantin back up to get help."

Jack straightened against his sapling and sucked in his stomach. "I'll go for help."

"No. Zorich is in good shape, and he knows his way around the forest." I rocked back on my heels and infused my voice with every ounce of authority I could muster. "Listen carefully. This is wilderness. If you get lost, prepare to die. We'd probably never find you, and there are grizzlies all through this country."

I paused to gauge their reaction, liking the stunned look they all shared, and then zipped the rucksack with my remaining supplies. "Stay right here." I nodded at the pile of provisions at my feet. "Here's food and water. I'll be down below, however far she's fallen, and I'll stay with her until medevac arrives. Zorich will let you know how she is when he gets back up here. The best way for you to help J.C. now is to stay put."

I slipped the pack on my shoulders as I rose from the ground. "Any questions?"

After focusing my sharpest I-mean-business stare on each in turn—Jack, Doubting Thomas, Lawrence Cameron and Margaret Armstrong—I discovered that sometimes intimidation works with adults, too. Without objection, all four accepted my explanation and my authority. I flashed them a brief reassuring smile. "All right, then. Stay together, and I'll be back as soon as J.C.'s taken care of."

Rather than follow Zorich's path and risk showering J.C. and Konstantin with earth and rock from above, I began my descent a few yards to the south, reverting to toddlerdom with a seated feet-first, butt-bumping slide that carried me over small rocks and through the steeper grassy spots. For braking, I dug in my heels and, as a precaution, made sure my hand hovered near some sturdy vegetation whenever possible. And about every ten feet, I scanned for their location, not bothering to hail them until I saw a flash of movement down below. Then I cupped my hands around my mouth to form a megaphone. "Have you found her?"

The words bounced between the steep walls of the gorge, the shout diminishing through echo and re-echo into stillness. The Russian's reply came in a single deep-throated bark aimed at the empty sky. "Yes!" A dozen yards below, a white flag whipped through the air. His handkerchief. I waved back, and then, crabbing heel and hand down the steep stony bank, I made my way to J.C.'s side.

She lay across the hill in a fetal curl, head slightly lower on the slope, a good position for combating the inevitable shock. Blood oozed from a nasty scrape on her forehead, trickling onto the parsley fern matted under her head. Dust dulled the brightness of her hair, and twigs adorned her crooked French braid. The violence of her fall had shredded the palms of hands now limp against the hill and bloodied the bruised knees which poked through torn pants. The Russian knelt by her ankles, tearing boughs of spruce from a branch as thick as my wrist. Slipping the rucksack from my shoulder, I crawled up beside him. "How is she?"

"Alive." He blew a stream of breath at a fly that buzzed his sweat-drenched nose and continued to strip the spruce. "But broken." He pointed a bough at her legs. "First we are making legs stiff. Then we are carrying her up the hill."

As gently as possible, I ran my hands over her legs. Except for the bloody knee, the right leg seemed fine, but swelling ballooned the left one just below the knee. A break, maybe a bad one.

After giving her midsection a visual check, I leaned close to her face until three poofs of breath had stirred against my cheek. Respiration seemed steady and strong. "What about her head and neck?"

He pulled the last bough from the spruce and started on a second branch. "I do not know. I am finding her just like this."

With my right thumb, I raised first one eyelid and then the other. Both pupils shrank to pin dots in the strong afternoon light. No concussion.

I sat back on my heels. "Reactions seem okay." As he reached for the next bough, I placed my hand on his, stopping him. "Let me do that, Konstantin. And I can splint her leg, too. What I can't do is get back to Wonder Lake as quickly as you can. As soon as you can find a ranger, they'll send a medevac." Confusion clouded his green eyes. "A helicopter."

He passed me the branch and glanced up the cliff. "Where?"

I patted the dirt beside me. "They'll pick her up right here."

In an instant, a smile chased the confusion out of his eyes. "Crazy Americans." His gaze swept across the new lake and then returned to my face. "Wonderful Americans." He took my hand, wrapping it inside one of his own, and held it against his chest. "Be brave, *krasavista.*" And then he dropped my hand, brushed gentle fingers against J.C.'s bruised cheek and, in a scramble of rocks, was gone.

Splinting her leg took all my concentration. A rigid

splint needs padding to cushion the injury from further damage. That meant tearing my knit cotton shirt into strips and then tying thick spruce boughs back onto the branch. Thank God for the layered look. To get the splints down the sides of the injured leg, I had to balance myself carefully, using my own body to hold the lower splint in position while carefully working the binding between the splint and my leg, then around both splints and her leg. With my outstretched uphill leg braced by the dug-in heel of my cocked downhill leg, I carefully positioned one spruce splint, snugging it into the groove between our legs, and then started on the binding. Within minutes, sweat stung my eyes and tension soured my stomach, but I kept at it, threading each wide band of cloth into position. Midway through the task, a hail floated down from above, but I ignored the rest of the crew. They had their orders: stay together and stay put. The muscles in my legs burned. My fingers fumbled. That same damned fly buzzed my head, too. Acid ate holes in my stomach, and one after another, the four bindings snaked into position, twin cloth tails awaiting the cinching knot that would secure the rigid splint against J.C.'s broken leg.

Before completing the job, I took a pair of cleansing breaths, inhaling deeply through my nose and then blowing gently through my mouth. Starting near the ankle, I overlapped the cloth tails, slowly slipping the knot into position against the spruce branch, and with a quick cinch, I tied it off once, twice. On the third binding, the one just below the fracture, J.C. moaned. On the fourth binding, the one just above the fracture, she screamed.

Her eyelids fluttered, and I levered myself off the ground, tucking my legs under me so I could again lean close to her face. "I won't hurt you any more, J.C."

Tearing another square of fabric from my shredded shirt, I soaked it with water from the pack and held it against her lips. "Help's on the way, J.C., but you've got to lie still and hang on a little longer."

As she sucked greedily at the sopping scrap of shirt, her eyes, bright with pain, finally stayed open, but her gaze darted wildly. I lowered my head until my face entered her field of vision. When she'd focused on me, I gave her my most reassuring smile. "You're doing great, J.C. Hurts like hell, I know. You're pretty banged up, but help's on the way."

Her lips stopped working the fabric of my shirt but only a croak emerged. "Don't try to talk." I wetted the cloth for her again and then gently placed my hand on her shoulder. "You're going to be just fine, J.C., and help is on the way."

Ever so slowly I withdrew from her field of vision, and her gaze drifted toward the placid water glinting below. Mine angled up the cliff and then surveyed the empty sky overhead. Under the circumstances, the waiting seemed like a detour to hell, one littered with stray thoughts of all that could go wrong. With the climbing season over, maybe the park no longer kept a helicopter on station for Denali rescues. Meaning rescuers would have to fly in from Talkeetna. Or possibly even one of the military bases in Anchorage. And once the medevac arrived, they'd still have to find us. Which wouldn't be easy since J.C.'s dive and my slide had coated us with layers of dust that effectively camouflaged us against the terrain. That thought finally got me moving again. After providing a fresh sucking rag to the injured woman, I made my way toward a bare patch of ground, determined to fashion some kind of signal to alert the helicopter to our position.

Turned out the medevac pilot didn't need the large triangle I'd fashioned from greenery to home in on us.

For a moment I confused the faint whup-whup-whup of rotors with the beating of my heart, but the confusion didn't last long. As the copter closed the distance, following first road and then creek, the roar of the engine built toward a crescendo as beautiful to me as any scored by Mozart. When the medevac surged over the dam at the end of the lake, I got to my feet, hooting as I swung the yellow pack over my head. The wash of the rotors shattered the mirrored surface of the water, and as the helicopter crossed overhead, a blast of air scoured dust, twigs and leaves from the surrounding ground.

The door slid open, and a figure sporting a helmet emblazoned with a red cross leaned out, clipped itself to the cable dangling from a winch fixed above the doorway and stepped into space. Within seconds of touchdown, a second helmeted figure reeled in the cable and rigged a stretcher for descent. On the ground the first figure snagged the stretcher, released the clip and then headed toward J.C. at a tilting but careful jog while the helicopter swung up and off.

That sight inspired a bit of panic on my part that left me bellowing at our rescuer. "Where's he going?"

With the flick of a wrist, the rescuer unfastened the chin strap and removed the helmet. A riot of black curls tumbled to her shoulders. "Just moving off a safe distance. Don't want to start another slide." Turning sideways, she brushed past me. "I'll need your help getting her into this basket."

After kneeling beside her patient, the paramedic spent about a minute assessing J.C.'s injuries, her voice a soothing murmur as she followed a drill similar to mine, starting with the head and finishing with the makeshift splint. For a moment she hesitated. Then she ran her hands along the padded branches, checking each of the binding knots, before waving for me. While I steadied the stretcher, balancing one side against an upraised knee, the paramedic lifted J.C. aboard, first settling head and shoulders, then carefully lifting her legs into position.

As her rescuer worked clips and belts to strap her in, J.C. managed to speak, her gaze fixed on my face and her voice a hushed sigh. "Pushed."

My heart somersaulted, and I leaned in close. "Say that again?"

A whisper. "Someone."

And another. "Pushed."

As the paramedic barked into a radio buttoned onto her shoulder, I studied J.C.'s face. Pain hollowed her cheeks, and fever dulled her blue eyes. "Someone pushed you? From up there?"

Last whisper. "Yes."

And then the paramedic leaned in front of me, reaching to tighten a nylon hood around J.C.'s head and shoulders as the helicopter moved above, buffeting us with the stiff wash of air from the rotors.

At her signal I released my grip on the stretcher. The basket slowly lifted from the wall of the gorge. The growl of the helicopter's engine echoed and re-echoed across the lake, the reverberation building an ache inside my head. I covered my ears and tried to watch the ascent of the stretcher, but the blast of air stung my eyes.

A hand closed on my elbow, and the paramedic signaled that I should put on her helmet and harness. I shook my head, holding up four stiff fingers while pointing to the forest above the gorge. She nodded her understanding, and after grabbing the empty cable snaking toward us, she clipped herself to the wire, gave me a thumbs-up and then started her ascent.

This time my eyes were drawn not to the helicopter hovering above but to the turbulent water of the lake below and the crack which had appeared in the dam. When the ground shook beneath my feet, I thought at first that the storm of echoing machine-made thunder had caused the shift. Even as the thought flitted across my mind, the crack in the dam widened, stretching into a gap, yawning into a crevasse as water found the channel and gushed through. As the dam dissolved, earth melting into the rushing water, I sank back against the steep slope, steadying myself with hands clutched to the scaled trunk of a white spruce still firmly rooted to the soil. By the time the helicopter's roar had dwindled to a fading whup-whup-whup, the waters of the creek once more ran free, leaving only the memory of J.C.'s whisper to assault my ears: someone pushed.

SOMEONE PUSHED. BUT WHY? AND
who? Both questions dogged me as I scrambled to the
top of the gorge to reunite with my companions. I
found them scattered under the trees in the lengthen-
ing shadows of late afternoon. Margaret Armstrong
propped herself against a mossy log. Her hands no
longer trembled, perhaps recovered now from the
shattering thrill of the push. She had spoken sharply
to J.C. earlier in the day. At the other end of the log,
Lawrence Cameron stared at nothing with the preoc-
cupied gaze of the genius. Had his earlier horror
resulted from J.C.'s fall or his own action? Perhaps he
feared losing a gifted student. Cradling his head upon
a bent arm, my pal Jack snored noisily beside a
thicket of ferns. Except for her graduate rank, J.C.
certainly matched the characteristics of the snotty
students he professed to hate. The very image of
unconcern, Thomas Hart bent over a pocket notebook, scribbling in the fading light. Perhaps he shoved
simply to spare the ranks of complex science from a

devotee who preferred the simplicities of children. Four possible *whos* and four possible *whys,* each more unbelievable than the last.

"You heard the helicopter, of course." I leaned over and nudged Jack's arm. He woke with a snort. "But did you realize the vibration from the rotor undermined the dam?" Another snort from Jack, a shrug from Doubting Thomas and shaken heads from the other two. "Well, the lake is gone."

That news stirred absolutely no interest from any of them. Tension's like that. Once the jittery edge breaks, a wave of fatigue numbs the survivors. An utterly subdued quartet followed me down the ridge, trailing behind one by one. There was no way I could imagine any one of them pushing J.C. Carr over that edge. And I certainly hadn't. Which left only Kontantin Zorich as a suspect, a thought I absolutely refused to entertain. From what I'd seen in our hours together, the Russian had way too much heart to ever inflict hurt.

To save time, I angled wide across the forest, aiming to intersect the road far closer to Wonder Lake than we'd left it. After the morning's paean to simplicity, maybe that's what was needed now. Maybe there wasn't a *who.* Maybe there'd been no push. After a fall like that, J.C. might have been delirious. And what if she turned out to be the kind of woman who had to assign blame for everything, even an act-of-God accident? I tried playing that soundtrack: "What, me slip? Ridiculous!" Although I didn't know her well, the imagined words seemed out of character for a young woman who'd needed time to think when asked if she was any good as a scientist. Still, no member of the quartet behind me seemed a likely heavy. And as for Konstantin Zorich, I'd already dismissed that possibility unequivocally.

After emerging from the trees and onto the gravel

road, we found ourselves less than a hundred yards from the shuttle-bus stop. As we neared camp, Boyce Reade came out to greet us. "The rangers received a transmission from the helicopter. Simple fracture of the tibia and, barring complications, they'll just keep her overnight."

"That's welcome news." Lawrence Cameron used a sleeve to blot the perspiration on his forehead. "Perhaps she'll feel up to attending the last day's session. She did work hard on her review."

"Are you out of your mind?" Thomas Hart propped his hands on his hips. "First Radishchev dies and now she's come damned close. With a trend like that, I'm not sure we should continue."

Margaret Armstrong did her best to skewer Doubting Thomas, but obviously her heart wasn't in it. "Are you suggesting we cancel a scientific conference on the basis of a two-incident trend to bad luck?"

Before the zoologist could respond, Boyce Reade stepped in to settle the argument. "We have no choice but to go on. When that dam let go, the flood water washed away a bridge and a large section of road. The park service says no one will be getting out of here for at least a couple of days."

In the hour before dinner, as I sluiced my dusty face under the spray of warm water from our temporary shower, I wrestled with the dilemma brought on by Thomas Hart's casual pairing of Arkady Radishchev's death and J.C. Carr's accident. How much more ominous would that "trend" seem if he knew that J.C. claimed her fall was no accident? But surely the means of both acts argued against any connection: the gun—my gun?—that killed Radishchev versus the shove—possible shove?—that injured Carr?

I lathered my arms with liquid soap, which left my skin tingling. But had she been shoved? That notion might be more a product of her injury than of reality.

And what possible motive could connect those two "victims"—an eminent Russian scientist justly receiving global acclaim and an uncelebrated American grad student recently considering aborting her career?

Toweling first my cropped hair and then my tingling body, I considered sharing J.C.'s claim and letting an objective third party weigh the evidence. Special Agent Malloy seemed an obvious choice, but her wild assertions had me spooked. After all, I'd been at the edge of that gorge when J.C. fell. Boyce Reade was another possibility, but hadn't he already suggested that a clever killer lurked among us? That left his objectivity in serious doubt. Even on short acquaintance, I trusted Konstantin Zorich. But he'd also been part of the hike. Plus the poor guy already had enough problems of his own.

By the time I massaged the last squirt of moisturizer into my left calf, I'd talked myself out of sharing J.C.'s claim or taking seriously Thomas Hart's suggestion of an ominous trend. The washed-out bridge clinched it for me. After all, why rush to judgment or make a hasty decision when we'd been left essentially trapped out here in the wilderness, at least for a couple of days?

After a robust meal of roasted duck with huckleberry sauce, Margaret Armstrong had recovered enough of her combative spirit to do battle with Doubting Thomas and provide the evening's after-dinner entertainment. She rose this time in defense of herself rather than Lawrence Cameron and proved that her instinct for self-preservation equaled her instinct to protect loyal friends. Most of the fifty guests had selected a brandy or liqueur from the half-dozen bottles arranged between the hurricane lamps on the sideboard and then carried their glasses back to the dining tables. Shaded oil lamps spilled puddles of light onto the tablecloths, suffusing the mess tent with a soft glow. A few die-hard smokers, including Jack McIntire, had stepped outside to satisfy their habit, but most of the guests talked quietly among themselves, filling the tent with a low hum of conversation. Although much had been made of the unfortunate coincidence of the Russian's death and the graduate student's fall, none of the guests seemed unduly concerned.

At the head of the tent, Boyce struggled to hang a portable screen. At the back, I fiddled with a projector, double-checking Margaret Armstrong's slides to make sure I got them in the carousel right-side-up and in the correct order. These days, photographic slides are as much a part of a biologist's equipment as the forceps, trowel, jars, alcohol, notebook and twenty-power hand lens that go into our field kits. While I fiddled, she waited at the dais, studying her notes and occasionally glancing up to check my progress. I pressed the *on* button, filling Boyce's screen with light and proving that someone had connected the long extension cord to the generator near the cook tent.

The flash of light caught the attention of Margaret Armstrong and our guests, who immediately stopped talking. At my signal, she donned a pair of glasses and plunged into the fray. "Lawrence Cameron suggested earlier today that, when at its best, science is simple enough to be comprehensible to a child. In that spirit, I intend this evening to demonstrate the method of evolution that Gaia implies. Species thrive not by killing each other off through competition but by cooperating with each other for the benefit of all."

Looking up from her notes, she paused and scanned the crowd for the first time, throwing a brief smile to Lawrence Cameron in the front row. Two tables behind Cameron, Thomas Hart fidgeted in his chair. She gave me the high sign, calling for the first slide, a picture of a single cell dotted with small green bodies. "This cell came from the leaf of a maple tree in my backyard in Washington. You'll recall Dr. Zorich described photosynthesis as inhaling carbon dioxide and exhaling oxygen. Please note the many chloroplasts in this cell which do that work."

She nodded in my direction, and I advanced the carousel, painting the screen with the green brilliance of another single-celled organism. In the seat between Cameron and Boyce Reade, Konstantin Zorich moved forward on his chair, intent on her words. "This form of bacteria is hardly more than a larger version of the chloroplasts in the cell from that maple leaf. Biologist Lynn Margulis showed us that such chloroplasts are the descendants of free living organisms similar to these bacteria."

With the wave of a hand, she called for another slide, this one showing three cells. Then she took up a wooden wand and advanced toward the screen to place the tip on a colorless cell. "Long ago, when the Earth was young, there lived single-celled organisms like this one." She moved the pointer to a green cell of bacteria. "In time, such organisms came upon and ingested free living bacteria like these." She moved the pointer to the last cell, colorless but dotted with tiny green bodies. "Most such competitive encounters led to the deaths of both. However some organisms survived, cooperating to their mutual benefit and living on as an entirely new species."

She dropped the pointer from the screen and faced her audience. "From just such encounters, the life on this planet grew, species by species, each descending from the same single-celled organism, the mother of us all. The lesson is clear: nature selects organisms for survival not on the basis of competition but on the basis of cooperation."

In his chair at the third table, Doubting Thomas positively squirmed, shaking his head and rattling his coffee cup. Margaret Armstrong ignored him, calling for a slide which paired the single colorless cell with the cloud-swirled image of Earth. "From the first single-celled organism of a young planet to the superorganism made up of Earth and her species that today we call Gaia, cooperation has guided evolution."

Thomas Hart now had his hand up, waving furiously, but Margaret Armstrong pretended not to see as she leaned her pointing wand against the dais. "Two great ideas gave birth to modern biology. First, that all life descended from unicellular organisms, and, second, that all organisms obey the laws of physics and chemistry. Now we have Gaia, the grand unifying theory of life on this planet, with Earth as a superorganism made up of all living things, which interact to maintain an environment conducive to life."

"Ridiculous!" Doubting Thomas jumped from his chair and banged a fist on the table, upsetting his table mate's drinks. "Who's the chairman of the Gaian regulatory board? Some paramecium from the rainforest? Do nematodes have a vote? How often do they meet to form committees to plan next year's temperature?"

In the front row, Konstantin Zorich moved to stand up, only to be restrained by Cameron's hand on his arm. I wanted to cheer both men—the Russian for having the passion to want to defend Margaret Armstrong and her associate for having the respect to let her fight her own battles.

She took her time about answering, pausing to replace her glasses in the bag at her feet and then to peer silently at her opponent. "Who chairs the regulatory board of the human circulatory system? Some erythrocyte carrying oxygen to the brain? Do the leukocytes have a vote? Our circulatory system provides a model for Gaia because the blood cells have a life of their own *and* work together to maintain the superorganism's life."

Thomas Hart opened his mouth to answer, but from the door of the tent, Jack McIntire jumped in. "Can the Earth truly be a living system without the ability to reproduce?" He shook the ice in his glass as he moved toward the sideboard. By my count, this glass of booze made three since dinner ended, but my friend showed no tremble of unsteadiness. "There is no mechanism for reproduction on a planetary scale."

"Not to our knowledge." She walked out from behind the dais. "Not to our current knowledge. But what if we do what James Lovelock suggests: flood the atmosphere of Mars with greenhouse gases to warm the surface and unfreeze the water? Then we could seed the planet with hardy arctic microorganisms to eat the carbon dioxide and produce oxygen to build an atmosphere. If we succeeded in creating life on Mars, would Earth have reproduced on a planetary scale?"

"Utterly absurd!" Doubting Thomas threw up his hands. "You have an answer for everything!"

"Of course!" She stiffened, and her voice shook. "That is my job. That is the scientist's task. For every question, an answer must be found."

Now Thomas Hart's voice shook. "Remember the Royal Society's credo: *Nullius inverba*. 'No man's word shall be final.'"

Margaret Armstrong rocked back on her heels, a sly smile ghosting her lips. "I am no man, and since the Royal Society failed to include me in their credo, I see no need to embrace it."

"Gotcha!" Jack McIntire rambled onto center stage, using the hand containing his glass to point at Doubting Thomas while throwing his free arm around Margaret Armstrong's shoulders. "Way to hold your ground, Maggie. Let that pompous prick fume while we have a toast."

He drew her against his side and raised his glass toward the assembled guests. Boyce threw me a glance over his shoulder, but how was I to intervene? Margaret Armstrong didn't seem disturbed, and Lawrence Cameron's smile positively beamed. Even Konstantin Zorich seemed delighted with Jack's spontaneity as the entire tentful of scientists rose to their feet, glasses in hand.

"To science." Jack lifted his glass, shaking the ice for emphasis. "To questions and to answers." He tossed off a healthy swallow. "I know I've found mine."

CHAPTER
13

A GUILTY CONSCIENCE TOOK MY MIND off theoretical aspects of biology, but by morning, questions of science returned to devil me—specifically, questions of ballistics and forensics. I spent a restless night worrying about my decision to keep quiet about J. C. Carr's claim that she'd been pushed into the gorge, and sometime after midnight, my fidgeting earned sharp words from my tent mate. I couldn't even assuage my insomnia with the paperback cure. Not only had Margaret Armstrong appropriated the book, she also decreed lights out at eleven P.M. As a hostess now literally trapped in the wilderness with a passel of guests and an uneasy conscience, I figured I was in no position to object to her highhandedness. When chorusing birds finally heralded the pink light of dawn, the fuzzy head I woke with lingered right through three cups of tea. Only a second run-in with the FBI finally cleared that up.

Special Agent Malloy broke the bad news just after breakfast when she waylaid me outside the mess tent, taking my elbow to draw me into private conversation as the conferees streamed by us. The results of the tests on Arkady Radishchev and my Colt .45 automatic were in. A single bullet that pierced his heart had killed the Russian, and my gun had fired the shot. "And although the bullet entered from the front, suicide seems unlikely. That wouldn't explain how the weapon found its way back into your holster."

My stomach heaved at her words, but I managed to hold on to my bagel and tea. After our first encounter, I knew just how to respond. "I don't think I should talk to you any more without my lawyer."

She jammed her hands into the pouch of her hooded sweatshirt and shrugged. "That's your prerogative, Mrs. Maxwell. The bridge washout spares me the need to remind you not to leave the park without informing me first."

Another flop of my stomach. She might have traded her dress-for-success blazer for grunge sportswear, but her words reminded me that she was all cop. Despite the seriousness of the moment, I tried to lighten things up. "I'll be sure to let you know when I make a run for it."

Her smile didn't reach her green eyes. "I don't consider you a flight risk. Jake and Jessie provide enough incentive for their mom to stick around."

My kids' names landed like a one-two punch. Jessie and Jake—how did Malloy know their names? Were her cohorts in Anchorage snooping around Eagle River, asking questions and starting rumors? Did my hero-hearted son know that his mom's gun was a murder weapon? Was my half-orphaned daughter worried that she might lose her mother, too? Simply asking those questions brought Jake and Jessie's grizzly-bear mother out of hibernation.

I grabbed Malloy, wrapping tight fingers around her upper arms. "Stay away from my children. You want someone to bully, come and find me. But leave my kids out of it."

Flexing her elbows, she lifted her arms, trying to break free, but I held on. "I'm warning you, Malloy. This is garbage, and you know it. And if you don't back off about my kids, I'll scream harassment and drag your ass into federal court for violating my civil rights."

Without waiting for a reply, I released her arms and stalked off, heading into the forest and away from the tents, needing a bit of time and privacy to sort things through. About fifty yards into the woods, I found a moss-covered log to lean against and sat down, breathing deeply to clear my head and calm my nerves. The dank earthiness of the shadowed forest soothed me. A late summer mosquito buzzed around my head, and a red squirrel chattered at my intrusion. I was too stunned to swat one or answer the other because all of my mental energy was focused on sending reassuring vibes to my kids back home in Eagle River. As for the questions that had transformed me into a griz, I'd soon have the answers because Travis MacDonald had scheduled his arrival at Kantishna's airfield for ten A.M. That left me little more than an hour to square things closer at hand.

Konstantin Zorich presented no problem. The Russian didn't retreat when he learned that my gun had killed his friend. On some level beyond words, he knew my innocence just as surely as I knew his. When I found him bent over the campaign table in his tent, scrawling words across the pages of a thick notebook, he showed no surprise at learning Malloy's news. Instead he capped his pen and regarded me with steady, serious eyes. "So clever, this killer, and yet I am wondering why? I think when we are finding why, we are also finding who." He took my hand and gave it a gentle squeeze. "And, until then, you are not to be worrying, Lauren. If this woman police is not finding killer, then we will."

While Zorich's reaction to Malloy's news that my gun was the murder weapon could be classified as calm determination, Boyce Reade's response would have to be termed agitated outrage. What seemed to really get him was the FBI agent's insinuation that I might be the killer. My boss grabbed my arm and literally dragged me out of the mess tent where I'd given him the high sign from the door. Out in the open air, he glanced once around the circle of tents and then dragged me some more, relenting only when we stood in the lee of the large cook tent. "Malloy suspects you?" He gave my arm a final shake and then freed me. "What on earth is she thinking?"

I couldn't resist a sigh. How in hell did I end up defending the FBI agent's twisted suspicions? "Malloy thinks I might have mistaken Radishchev for a grizzly."

"Bullshit!" The word cracked out of Boyce Reade like a rifle shot, ominous and full of fury. "Utter, unadulterated bullshit!" His gray eyes stormed. "I never should have told Coppola about your gun."

Seemed like a rewrite of history to me, but at the moment I didn't care. Boyce Reade's reaction was the blue-blood equivalent of an alpha grizzly's rampant and roaring readiness to fight to the death. In that moment I forgave him for roping me into the conference, volunteering my services for Margaret Armstrong's hunt and suggesting I leave Alaska for our nation's capital. He asked for no explanation and exhibited no doubts. What a boss!

Buoyed by the trust of both men, I trotted to Kantishna's airfield a half hour later with the *Rocky* theme music playing in my head. Malloy's crackpot scenario no longer had me spooked. Neither Konstantin Zorich nor Boyce Reade had found her theory persuasive. I hadn't figured out how my gun came to be the murder weapon—not yet, at least—but my admittedly elementary grasp of criminal law reassured me that judges found such circumstantial evidence a fundamentally unsound basis for determining guilt. With that fresh spurt of confidence and a welcome resupply of hardware from Travis, I'd be ready to take on Malloy and the killer and the whole damned world.

Travis MacDonald's Cessna 206 swooped across the majestic backdrop of the Alaska Range right on time and circled the airfield at Kantishna, an old mining district that was absorbed into the park in the early 1980s. As the plane lined up for landing, I battled a flicker of panic. At one time Trav jockeyed jets on and off aircraft carriers and still easily qualified for rescue work with the Civil Air Patrol out at Elmendorf Air Force Base. Despite those impressive credentials, my heart still kicked into a trot when a drop in the pitch of his engine signaled his final approach. Max had been a hell of a pilot, too, but that didn't matter in the end. A stray wind shear, the failure of a fatigued engine mount, intersecting with the flight path of a flock of geese—such are the utterly random and seemingly minor events that create absolute catastrophes in the age of flight. Life is nothing more than a crapshoot. I really hadn't believed that until Max persuaded me to learn how to fly. By the time I got my license, I understood that pilots exist a mere eyeblink removed from disaster, knowledge that lent a special edge to my wholehearted love of flying even before Max went down in our plane. After his disappearance, I'd climbed right back in a cockpit for a solo flight, knowing I had to fly again immediately or risk losing my nerve forever. Allowing my kids back in the air took a lot more time, but in the past three months, both had flown as passengers again.

As the white turboprop taxied off the field, Trav poked an arm out of his window and gave me a vigorous thumbs-up. A few minutes later the Cessna rolled to a stop, and, when the top of his red Brillo pad hair emerged from the plane, I shouted a welcome. "That was one smooth landing."

Using the wing as a monkey bar, he swung out of the plane and onto the paved field, spreading his arms for a welcome hug. "Yup." He gave me two quick squeezes. "That's one from Jake and one from Jessie."

I squeezed him back. "How are they?"

"Pesky as hell." After releasing me, he tugged a crushed Red Sox cap from his back pocket and settled it on his pad of hair. "Finally got your computer dialed into the Net, and now they're racing to see who can be the first to dig up an e-mail pal on each continent. Jake's got a six-to-five lead, and they're jamming my mailbox with updates."

He reached into the plane for the first of the baggage, and I lined up beside him, ready to take the toss. "Sounds like Jake won. They won't find anybody to correspond with in Antarctica."

Trav heaved a bulging backpack out the narrow door, which I intercepted and lowered to the ground. "Don't underestimate your son. He hooked in to the Coast Guard, which runs America's installations down there. The coasties told him the Argentines actually had some kids born at their base. So now he's negotiating for a courier."

He drew out the long, gray hard-plastic case of a rifle that I handled with special care. "If he put that much effort into his math, he'd get in to MIT."

Travis paused long enough to throw me a nasty look over his shoulder. "The kid just turned twelve, Lauren. Let's not rush him."

At one time I would have bristled at hearing words

like that from a friend but no longer. Travis MacDonald had earned the right to butt in with Jake. He had flown more hours looking for Max's plane than any other CAP pilot, and when the search ended, the soft-hearted stranger had stayed around to rescue my son. Trav hates credit cards, time clocks, sermons, mortgages, political parties and television. He lives in a cabin on fifty acres near Eklutna that features the Great Land's biggest bathtub and finest collection of jazz. And he gives my Jake the one thing I'm unable to provide—a terrific model of what it takes to be a man.

I ducked under the wing and leaned my head on his shoulder. "You're right. Why rush him? By the time he's ready for college, MIT will probably offer a correspondence diploma over the Net."

He grabbed a foot-square cardboard box and drew it out of the plane, opening the top to reveal something white and curly. "Is this really what you wanted?"

I reached into the box and lifted out the sheep's head, admiring the dark marble eyes and almost-looked-real horns that curled full circle. Stuffed animals are the humane alternative for trophy hunters. "Yup. I promised I'd help Margaret Armstrong bag a trophy-class Dall ram, but I never specified the kind of trophy I had in mind."

He stroked the polyester fleece with one knuckly finger. "She'd have to be a pretty dizzy dame to go for this. Most of the guys I've flown on trophy hunts would not be amused."

I lowered the sheep's head back into the box. "She's not a guy, Trav. That's what I'm counting on."

He pulled one last bit of baggage from the plane, a red zippered pouch about the size of a file folder. "Special delivery, although I'm not sure I approve."

I welcomed the weight of the pouch in my hands

and unzipped it slowly. The hard metal inside cooled my palm and fingers as they slid into place around the butt. When I drew my hand out of the red pouch, the sun silvered the barrel of the Smith and Wesson .38 revolver. For the first time since turning my Colt over to Denali Park's chief ranger, my heart felt light, a realization that left me with a bittersweet pang. How had I gotten to this place where a lethal weapon seemed a wonderful and terrible and natural extension of my self?

Travis MacDonald studied the gun in my hand. "That's not much of a stopper for a grizzly."

I snapped open the cylinder, giving it a spin. "Only has to stop a human."

He raised his eyes to meet my own. "Will you please tell me what the hell is going on?"

CHAPTER

14

TRAVIS MACDONALD IS A REASONABLE
man. He wanted to know what was going on, and I
promised him a long story. At that news, he raised a
traffic-cop hand. "Then hold it till we get more
comfortable." He swung the pack onto his back and
tucked the rifle case under his arm. "Let me get
settled at the roadhouse, then we'll grab a beer and a
soak."

I slipped the gun into the plastic pouch, zipped it
shut and slid my weapon into the box containing the
stuffed sheep's head. "Little early for a beer, isn't it?"

Trav checked the position of the sun and grinned.
"Looks like daylight to me. Bet they've got iced tea for
you temperance types."

Kantishna's roadhouse dated from prospecting
days at the start of the twentieth century, when a few
thousand miners braved Denali's bears and isolation
to pan for gold and silver. By the 1980s the town
found itself absorbed into the park and prohibited

from mining, so property owners turned to tourism, renting out cabins and heated tents to vacationers who gathered for family-style meals in a communal lodge. When I'd explained to Trav the crush of guests at Wild America's camp, he'd opted instead for Kantishna's oldest inn, which features that Left Coast essential—a hot tub. Within an hour of his arrival at the airfield, we'd eased into hot bubbling water that reached our chins.

Trav took a long pull on his micro-brew beer and then carefully set the bottle on the wooden deck surrounding the sunken hot tub. "Your need of that gun have anything to do with the Russian who turned up dead a couple of days ago?" When I allowed as how it did, he vaulted straight to the heart of the matter. "So where's your .45?"

I leaned my head against the rim of the tub and turned my attention to the downy clouds drifting in from the west that snagged on the jagged peaks ringing Denali Park. "FBI's got it."

Trav gave me a count of three before running out of patience. "You going to tell me a story or make this a question-and-answer session?"

I decided to give it to him straight and looked him right in the eye. "It looks like the Russian was killed with my gun. The ranger took the .45 the first day, and the FBI agent on site is test marketing a bunch of scenarios that make me the shooter."

He didn't even blink. "How come?"

"Because my gun's the murder weapon."

Now he blinked. Twice. "You're kidding?"

I sighed deeply. "I'd love to be able to kid about this, Trav, especially since the other Russian assures me she ran the same gag on him. But I'm afraid I lost my sense of humor when Special Agent Malloy mentioned Jake and Jessie. Gag or not, she's checking up on me, and I'm not talking to her again without a lawyer."

He scooped up his bottle of beer for another long pull. "The cop in charge is a woman? Think that explains this?"

I nodded and slid a little deeper into the water, not caring if I dunked the tendrils of hair on my neck that had escaped my hairdresser's razor. Few women like to admit it in these emancipated days, and yet sometimes the biggest threat to our advancement comes not from men determined to keep us down but from highly competent professional women unwilling to give up the "someone special" label that comes from being as good as the guys. The good news is that hardly anybody's surprised to see a boss-woman in charge these days. The bad news is that the high achievers who made the early breakthroughs are feeling taken for granted. I know that I am. Which is good, really, because we'll all be better off when competence in women is taken for granted. Still, a big part of my identity's tied up with being smarter, bolder, tougher and all the other -er's than women are supposed to be. I always stood out because there wasn't a crowd. Now there is, and sometimes I get so sore, dammit, that I'd like to stomp a few of these gals who think they're so smart. That urge might explain some of Malloy's blind animosity.

Trav drained the last of his beer. "So what's the deal with the dead guy?"

I stopped the pop psychologizing about Malloy's motives and focused on the real problem, offering a quick review of the few—amazingly few—things that were known about the death of Arkady Radishchev. "He was a famous scientist. I mean world class. First trip to the U.S., came with a Siberian colleague, spent a night walking in from the Eielson, wound up dead just beyond the tents, one shot through the heart from my gun."

Trav arched an eyebrow. "Tell me about the Siberian."

An uncontrollable flash of heat reddened my cheeks, and he raised the other eyebrow. "Konstantin Zorich didn't do it. That's not just my opinion. My boss assures me that killing Radishchev would be like an American killing Thomas Edison or a Pole killing the pope. In other words, no chance. My gut tells me the same."

For a long moment Trav didn't reply. With a sudden motion, he ducked under the surface and then came up for air, streams of water cascading around his ears and nose. "So you figure the killer's part of the conference, which is why you wanted a gun."

Not a question but a statement of fact. And I realized in that moment that Trav MacDonald had it exactly right. I did figure the killer was part of the conference, even though I hadn't been conscious of coming to that conclusion. And that was why I wanted my other gun—for protection from the human threat, not the bears. On that first day, the day of Arkady Radishchev's death, Boyce Reade had suggested that the killer was hiding among us. Sometime between then and now, I'd decided my boss was right. And all the time, while I'd been hostessing on a conscious level, my inner sleuth had been on the case.

A thrill of recognition zapped through me with the force of an electric shock. I sat up straight, letting my bare shoulders rise above the bubbling surface of the hot tub, and finally answered my pal. "That's right. I do think the killer is part of the conference. But to figure out who, I have to know why. 'Love, lust, loathing or lucre, the four *L*'s of murder'—P. D. James says those are the basic motivations for murder. 'And the greatest of these is lucre.' But none of them fit Radishchev's death. Everyone here is a scientist. Why would one scientist knock off another?"

"Lucre?" Trav grinned and rolled his eyes. "There's a word you don't run into except on PBS. And nobody greedy for money goes into science, anyway. What about revenge? Jealousy? Blackmail? Ambition? Rivalry?"

"Not revenge." I gave my head one emphatic shake. "The victim is a Russian on his first trip to America. He didn't have time to diss someone badly enough to draw deadly retaliation."

"What about the other Russian?"

Trav asked the question with an even and neutral tone of voice. My answer came out pretty shrill. "I already told you. He didn't do it."

Trav wasn't about to let me off the hook. "I heard you the first time, Lauren. What I didn't hear was a concrete explanation of why he didn't do it. He's the obvious suspect because he knew the guy. Most killers know their victims and kill for a reason. Money, revenge, jealousy, blackmail, ambition or rivalry— any one of them is believable with the best of friends. And all of them are a stretch with a stranger."

Far be it from me to prefer a yes man to the more difficult but sincere friendship of a helpmate like Travis MacDonald. Friends like Trav keep you honest. In a world built on shifting moral sands, they are the necessary bedrock that keeps one ethically grounded. Only a fool prefers to twist unpleasant facts and ignore unpopular ones in an effort to recast a painful reality to fit the form of a preferred version of events. Not that Trav's doubts had changed my mind. I *knew*—inside and out—that Konstantin Zorich hadn't killed Arkady Radishchev. But I'd just learned that convincing Travis MacDonald would take more than simply my word. I'd intended to tell Trav about

J. C. Carr's claim that she'd been pushed, but that could wait. Allaying his suspicions concerning the Russian took precedence.

I grabbed the towel from the edge of the hot tub and draped it across my chest. "Let's go find Konstantin Zorich, and you can decide for yourself."

Each day the conferees had an hour of free time after the midday meal for catching up on notes, polishing scheduled papers or grabbing naps. Locating Konstantin Zorich required locating Lawrence Cameron, and he could usually be found on the shore of Wonder Lake in an elemental bask of earth, air and water in mountain, sky and lake. He raised a hand in greeting and Zorich flashed a smile as Trav and I approached and exchanged introductions.

Cameron sat on a thick mat of grass, one arm clasped around his bent knees while his free hand plucked fresh-picked blueberries from the bag at his side. "Have some?"

Trav sank to the grass beside him, legs crossed Indian style, and scooped a shallow handful of berries. "From what Lauren says, meeting you is like meeting Einstein, and I know if I had that privilege, I'd want to ask him about relativity. Would you be offended if I asked you to explain your theory of Gaia?"

The breath snagged in my throat as I settled down beside the Russian, but Cameron didn't mind. "I just read of a New York businessman, Wall Street fellow with a pinstripe suit and conservative raincoat, who stopped on the sidewalk a queer-looking nineteenth-century sort of man wearing a flat-brimmed hat and a magnificent beard. 'I'll give you five minutes,' the businessman said. 'Tell me what you believe.' Strikes me as an eminently practical approach. Rather flattering to be asked."

He flashed a quick smile at Trav before beginning

the tutorial. "Gaia takes us back to the time when scientists accepted the idea of a living earth. In 1785 the father of geology, James Hutton, told the Royal Society of Edinburgh that he considered the Earth a superorganism and the proper course of its study to be physiology." Cameron lifted berry-stained fingers toward the sky and the water and the mountain. "The atmosphere, he said, is the respiratory system, the rivers and oceans are the circulatory system and the rocks are the bones. I would add that the ecosystems are the organs."

Trav pointed at Denali. "That big piece of granite isn't alive."

"Quite right." Cameron nodded his approval. "But consider what American physicist Jerome Rothstein notes of your great redwood trees, *Sequoia gigantea*. A hundred meters tall, two thousand tons, three thousand years old and fully ninety-five percent of it dead wood and bark with only a thin layer of cambium and xylem living. Do you consider that redwood to be dead?"

Trav grinned. "Sounds like a trick question to me."

Cameron tossed back his head and laughed. "Not at all, my friend. That big piece of granite you call Denali by itself isn't alive. Yet when coupled with plate tectonics and the hydrological cycle, that granite provides part of the living earth's nutrition, replenishing vital elements for the biota. Species and environment are inseparable. Together they form the living earth and together they work to optimize conditions for life. That is Gaia."

Trav cocked his head and frowned. "Bet the Creationists love you."

"Hardly. Gaia is too elemental and pagan for the fundamentalists. Smacks of alchemy and *Anima Mundi* and the goddess. Blasphemy, in a word." Cameron sighed and shook his head. "Not that we get much credit from their opponents, either. In its titanic battle with the know-nothings, science has become as imperious and arrogant as her enemies. Perfectly sensible scientists insist that Gaia posits a universe ruled by a godlike intelligence."

Konstantin leaned forward. "Perfectly sensible scientists find no intelligence outside the mind of man."

Travis squarely faced the Russian for the first time. "Do you find intelligence outside the mind of man?"

Cameron looked from Trav to Konstantin and then shot a glance at me. I shrugged a response as the Russian lifted the cone of a spruce from the grass. "This is my study, and what am I learning? That in drought, a tree is dropping needles to conserve water. That with beetles, a tree is creating more sap to plug the holes. To respond purposively to the environment—is that not intelligence?"

Cameron raised his eyes toward Denali. "Just as there is life beyond the human species, so there is an intelligence beyond the human mind. Life is planetary—species and environment, evolving together. The mountain is just as much a part of Gaia as we are—inseparable parts which add up to a greater whole. Sounds rather nice, actually, but not a bit like God. Can't imagine why all these fellows object."

CHAPTER
15

LESS THAN AN HOUR LATER, THE OBJEC-
tions were mine when Trav MacDonald suggested
Konstantin Zorich and I skip the afternoon session of
the conference so we could help him locate a trophy-
class Dall ram for Margaret Armstrong to kill. I didn't
object to flying, just to the first stop, a destination that
didn't become apparent until the Cessna left the
ground. They'd gone on ahead to the airfield while I
returned to my tent to change into something warmer,
arriving at my digs before Margaret Armstrong woke
from her siesta.

Ever try pawing through a suitcase without making
a sound? The wood floor of the platform tent creaked
as I dug through my clothes, searching for jeans, T-
shirt, hiking and slick socks, fleece pullover and taslan
anorak. I'd secured the last knot on my boots when I
remembered my spare gun. After digging the zippered
plastic pouch out of the bottom of my suitcase, I
stuffed the .38 in my knapsack, tossed in a box of
ammunition, crammed my holster and gunbelt in on

top and bolted out the door. A half hour, I'd promised them, and a glance at my watch told me I had just under twenty minutes to make the airfield. Shouldering the knapsack, I set off at an easy lope.

Trav revved the engine at the sight of me, and I kicked into a faster pace, ducking under the wing just as the plane started rolling forward. Konstantin reached out a hand for my knapsack and, after throwing that on the opposite seat, grabbed my arm and hauled me up and into the plane.

While I buckled myself in, he moved into the co-pilot's seat and then half-turned to face me. "Such a thing for one man to be owning! And did you see? Wheels and skis to be landing on ground and snow!"

I nodded. "It's amazing how they rig these planes up for any eventuality. Too bad we can't try them both, eh, MacDonald?"

"Oh, but we can!"

Before I could point out the lack of snow, I noticed that both his and Konstantin's eyes had been drawn to Denali, radiant in the midafternoon sun. Both men gazed at the mountain with the longing eyes of a passionate lover. Didn't need a degree in rocket science to figure that one out. "You can't be serious!"

The plane picked up speed, jouncing a little as it barreled down Kantishna's runway. "Travis MacDonald, this is not the right season for a glacier landing! The surface is just too damned soft."

Travis eased the stick forward, sending us hurtling across the ground. "Not always. No harm in looking, is there?"

The Russian finally turned to face me again, the passion in his eyes replaced by a gleam of excitement. "As my friend, Travis, is saying: mountain is sturdier than aircraft carrier bobbing at high seas!"

Talk about closed minds. They'd obviously made their decisions and cared not a whit for my opinion.

So I didn't offer anything further and instead relaxed into my seat, determined to enjoy the flight.

Funny thing about flying—I still love it, despite Max's death. When his plane went down, I never seriously considered giving up my pilot's license. In Alaska, flying is a necessity, not a luxury. Long distances and few roads leave flying the only way to reach most of the state. Not that my continued flying doesn't seem odd to lots of people. Their refrain goes something like this: 'If I'd lost a loved one the way you did, I don't think I could ever fly again.' Try substituting drive for fly. Far more people die in car wrecks than plane crashes, but no one expects their survivors to stop driving. And so, despite Max's death, I still fly and still love it. Strap me in an airplane, get those engines screaming, launch fuselage and passengers into the air at hundreds of miles an hour—I love it. The little dips and curls of turbulence don't bother me, and I don't get sick. I never tire of looking out the window. From the inside of an airplane looking out, the bird's-eye view offers a magical panorama of terrain—valleys cut by ribbons of water and bounded by soaring peaks—and also of atmosphere—clouds of every description, from gossamer wisps to brooding thunderheads, all topped by blue skies and brilliant sunshine. What's not to love? And I never tire of watching the ground below, tracing my path across terrain that finally looks just like the maps in all those geography texts of my childhood. Which is exactly how I planned to content myself when Trav's Cessna left the ground.

Outside the small window, a shag of trees whizzed by. Inside the small plane, the skin on Trav's jaw tightened as our speed increased, and the Russian's dark eyes sparkled. In a small plane, one can feel that tiny, endless, sensual moment when the friction stops and the flight begins, that millisecond of time when everything's in flux, neither grounded nor airborne, one last little tug and then release. At that moment my heart literally lightens and almost seems to take flight along with the plane. This time was no different. As Trav's plane slipped the bonds of friction, a smile spread across my face.

Trav banked the Cessna in a slow circle and then throttled back to cruising speed as he aimed the nose of the plane at the Muldrow Glacier and answered Konstantin's stream of questions. I pressed my nose to the window, eager to fly the terrain I'd traced so often with a finger on a map. Most Denali flights follow the U-shaped glacial valleys, soaring above the humped ridges and gaping crevasses created by the flow of those rivers of ice. In the next few minutes, the lake- and bog-studded valley gave way to sparsely forested foothills, which in turn gave way to rocky alpine tundra dusted with fresh snow and dotted with a patchwork of piles of last season's snow, still melting in deeply shadowed corners. The sun had climbed high enough to light the ground and, when at last we reached the Muldrow's true ice field flowing between knife-edged ridges of granite, the dazzle from below nearly blinded.

I leaned forward and touched Trav's shoulder. "Where do we land?"

He cocked his head in my direction. "Want to try the Kahiltna?"

"God, no, that's a public latrine!"

Konstantin frowned, mulling that over for a moment, before asking the obvious question. "What are you saying?"

"I'm saying that ten thousand people have now reached Denali's summit. All of those people pooped on the mountain. And the climate being what it is, all that poop's still up there."

My Russian glanced at Travis. "Poop?"

Trav flashed a grin to both of us. "She's not kidding about the latrines, Zorro. On Kahiltna they've got 'em at base and at roughly fourteen thousand. On the West Buttress at about seventeen thousand, the rangers have designated a crevasse to receive the liners from each group's shitter."

Konstantin glanced at me. "Shitter?"

"Slang for 'poop.'" I tossed a grin back at Trav. "I think a visit to Kahiltna would be less than aesthetic for our Russian guest."

Trav nodded his agreement. "Then the Ruth Glacier it is. We'll try for the Sheldon Amphitheater."

Alaska's original glacier pilot was Don Sheldon, a bush flyer of enduring legend. When rescue demanded he land in a narrow river canyon, he set his plane down going upstream on the only possible stretch and then floated back down to take off over the same water. In pioneering Denali flight, he used spruce boughs to solve the problem of depth perception on a field of solid white. In the 1960s, Don Sheldon set the standard that 1990s pilots still try to uphold.

Trav changed our flight path into a moderate climb, going for altitude to lift us over the ridges that girded all of the glaciers. In a matter of minutes, we'd again torn free of the earth, sailing high over a sea of snowy peaks, granite whitecaps that never moved. Above it all rose Denali, broad-shouldered and proud, and just to the south, Mt. Foraker. I pointed to the smaller mountain. "That peak's known as Sultana, Denali's wife."

He spared Foraker a glance, but the mountain quickly drew him back. "When Russia was owning Alaska, we are calling the mountain *Bulshaia Gora*—Home of the Sun."

Trav steered the plane into a tight circle around the south peak and below us lay the gleaming expanse of the Kahiltna Glacier, preferred launching point for commercial expeditions. "Got a fair bit of new snow, but you can make out the outlines. Of the airstrip—there. And just beyond, see where the medicos set up camp?"

Depressions in the fresh snow clearly marked what in late spring and early summer is a high-altitude village. At the question in Konstantin's dark eyes, I jumped in. "Each year they set up a lab to study the effects of cold and altitude. Most recently, a pharmaceutical firm provided funding so they could run tests on a new drug for emphysema."

Our flight path headed away from the mountain's peak, angling east to get lined up for the Ruth Glacier, yet another of Denali's five rivers of flowing ice. Basically, glaciers are a mechanism for moving snow from places where it accumulates faster than it can melt to places where snow melts faster than it can accumulate, and for unexplained reasons, glaciers can surge hundreds of feet in one day. In 1956 the Muldrow beached a block of ice that melted into Wonder Lake. On that run, the Muldrow moved forward as much as 1,100 feet in a day and advanced a total of four miles before dormancy returned. In summer, tight corners tear the ice, creating crevasses. The Sheldon Amphitheater offered a wide spot in the ice unlikely to be creased by crevasses and therefore safe for landing.

Trav eased the Cessna a bit lower, swooping in over the Ruth Glacier and starting a landing approach. For some reason my normal exhilaration at landing failed to arrive. Part of my mind had exited the present and gone off in search of an elusive thought that nagged at me from just out of reach. Even the magnificent vista of rock and ice failed to capture my full attention.

Konstantin pointed to a cascade of rock and ice that skittered down the eastern ridge of the amphitheater. The kiss of the sun had launched mini-avalanches. On a warm day the surface temperature can reach fifty degrees, and with the reflecting glare, the sun literally blisters unprotected skin. That same heat melts the ice and snow, undercutting top-heavy cornices. Konstantin opened his mouth to comment, but before he could get the words out, an awesome tableau transfixed us all.

High atop one serrated ridge, an enormous block of ice tottered. The shriek of shattering ice drowned the whine of the engine, and a banshee wail penetrated the closed cabin of the plane. The house-size ice tilted, breaking free from the ridge and sliding down the sheer face. Striking a ledge, the block split into smaller pieces the size of trucks and cars, which catapulted into space, trailed by lacy tendrils of snow. And then, one by one, those huge blocks of ice returned to earth in a barrage that cratered the entire width of the Ruth Glacier, including the Sheldon Amphitheater, and raised blinding clouds of snow.

Now *that* got my attention, and the elusive thought I'd been seeking escaped me once and for all.

The acrobatic ice grabbed Trav's attention, too. He eased back on the stick, lifting the nose of the Cessna toward the mountain's peak again. "Snow may be a little too soft for a glacier landing today."

For the next few minutes, I tried to rewind my thoughts to the place where I'd finally lost the one that had nagged. But the thought that had been ghostly and out of reach was now absolutely gone. I decided to just forget it, figuring it couldn't have been that important, anyway. As I would learn to my regret, I couldn't have been more wrong.

CHAPTER 16

AFTER LEAVING THE RUTH GLACIER, the Cessna again soared around the south peak of Denali, then Trav headed his bird due west in search of Dall sheep. Konstantin offered me the binoculars, but I shook my head, preferring to study the land without benefit of the glasses. At one point he spotted a band of fifty ewes and lambs, all moving together into the lower elevations, beginning the great migration from the river headwaters of their summer range to the windswept northern ridges of their winter range.

Trav dipped a wing, taking the Cessna into a looping descent that brought us over the sheep. Even without the glasses, a young lamb could be seen gamboling at the back of the flock, lagging in his ewe's shadow. And then a larger shadow darted across the autumn grass as a golden eagle swooped out of a hidden aerie, intent on claiming his prey.

As our airplane slid by, the bird attacked feet-first, claws spread to sink into the lamb's hide like grappling hooks. Despite the powerful beating of his massive wings, the eagle could not lift his prize. Seeing the predator's distress, the ewe galloped forward, now ready to harry the eagle to save her youngster. In an instant the eagle released the prey that had anchored him in harm's way, gliding only as far as a nearby rock. After nudging the lamb into motion, the ewe chased him back to the safety of the herd, but the splash of crimson now staining his coat identified him among the many.

The incident upset me, providing a vivid reminder of the vulnerability of all species of youth in a world populated by all manner of predators. Not for the first time that weekend, I wanted—no *needed*—to connect with my own pair of lambs. Touching base with Jake and Jessie through Travis was just not good enough. Although he'd assured me the two were oblivious to Arkady Radishchev's death and unaware of any inquiries made by the FBI, I needed to hear that directly from my kids. As soon as the Cessna rolled to a stop back at Kantishna's airfield, I popped open the door, swung myself to the ground and headed for the pay phone at the roadhouse, leaving Trav and Konstantin to tie down the plane.

Jessie answered on the third ring, trilling a cheerful hello. I tried to match my voice to hers. "Hey, baby, whatcha doing?"

"Hi, Mom!" Her greeting carried real enthusiasm, and so did the announcement she made to the rest of the clan at Eagle River, every word of which came through to Kantishna. "Hey, Jake, Nina—Mom's on the phone." She turned her attention back to me. "I'm filling out forms."

I leaned against the wall, settling in for a cozy chat. "What kind of forms, sweetie?"

"Soccer forms." Her voice brightened even more. "They want me to play on an all-star team! Some of the kids had to try out but not me. Coach said he already knew I was the best eight-year-old sweeper in Anchorage."

The creak of the stairs leading to the roadhouse porch warned me that I'd soon have company. "When did all this happen?" And why hadn't Trav warned me?

"Just today. Coach came to my game and talked to Nina." Her voice deflated just a bit. "She said I'd have to wait for you to sign the forms. You'll sign, won't you, Mom? You can call Coach, and he'll explain everything."

Bless Nina, my house mate, for her diplomacy. Too bad I had nothing better to offer than the usual parental dodge. "We'll see about that when I get home."

"Aw, Mom—"

Before Jessie could finish her complaint, Jake's voice floated over the telephone line. "Put a sock in it, squirt. Anyway it's my turn to talk."

Anticipating my objection to his phone snatch, his first words into the receiver offered an explanation. "I am so sick of hearing about all-star soccer I could puke." An illness no doubt complicated somewhat by envy since I'd refused a similar offer on Jake's behalf when he was Jessie's age. "Wait'll the season starts. That coach has a bunch of major whiners on his team. I'll bet even Little Miss Perfect Jessie will get into the act."

At that moment Trav and Konstantin plowed through the door, both men spotting me at the pay phone at the end of the hall. After pantomiming the draining of a very large glass, Trav led the Russian into the tap room while I continued to connect with my happy home with a bit sterner tone of voice. "That's not very nice, kiddo. I don't expect third-grader garbage from you."

Deep sigh. "Sorry. It's just that she's a broken record."

In the distance, the broken record added a new refrain. "Tell Mom we won't be able to go camping next weekend. I've gotta go to a soccer clinic."

My, how priorities change. At that moment mine did, too, moving from daughter to son. "What about you, Jake? Heard from your new coach yet?"

"Yeah. He says we already got a goalie so I'll have to find a new position."

"Terrific!" The enthusiasm in my voice wasn't faked. "You've been a good goalie, sweetie, but watching you guard that net has taken years off my life. Wait'll he sees you run. I'm betting the megawatt kid will impress the heck out of his new coach."

After a bit more boosting of adolescent male ego and a quick exchange with Nina, who confirmed my kids' blissful ignorance of the death at the Gaia conference, I joined the men in the taproom for a quick happy-hour beer. Konstantin and I timed our return to the Wild America camp to arrive at the dinner hour. As we walked down the Kantishna Road, the aromas of baking bread and seafood simmering in a delicate tomato sauce wafted out of the camp to tempt us and any bears in the vicinity. The chef's menu featured a San Francisco cioppino, mixed greens with vinaigrette and garlicky sourdough rounds to be served with a chilled California chardonnay. My stomach growled. If a grizzly did show up, the bear would have a fight on his claws before I'd give up my portion.

By the time we arrived at the mess tent, only the table shared by Thomas Hart and Jack McIntire had two chairs still unoccupied. Konstantin and I joined that unlikely pair, exchanging smiles and pleasantries, before sampling the fare. Each table setting included a roomy salad plate mounded with mixed greens, a small bread plate and a wide shallow bowl for the cioppino. A chef's helper I recognized from the first morning trotted baskets of sourdough rounds to each of the tables while two other young men ladled the thick red seafood stew from deep tureens. Conversation continued while we waited for the waiters to reach our table. Only Doubting Thomas started his dinner, eagerly spearing the greens and chopped vegetables from his salad plate. By the time the cioppino arrived, he'd polished off much of the opener.

"Looks like you've got an appetite to match McKinley." Jack McIntire nudged his salad plate in Hart's direction. "Have mine, too. Mother never could get me to eat my vegetables."

"No thanks." Hart frowned and wrinkled his nose. "Radishy thing leaves kind of a bitter aftertaste." He tore off a piece of sourdough and washed it down with a big slug of ice water. "That's better. I think."

Just then the waiter arrived with the cioppino, and everyone oohed and aahed as he ladled shrimp, scallops and clams, along with Dungeness crab and halibut, into our bowls. The men lifted their spoons without delay. I closed my eyes and inhaled the tomatoey sea fragrance, reminding me of many wonderful meals with Max when we lived by San Francisco Bay; meals shared even before we fell in love. Before kids, before marriage, before even love, there is lust, and the memory of that, more than anything, was what filled my mind. The power of our passion had never dimmed. Marriage and kids added complexity to our passion, but in the end, Max and I didn't have enough time together to completely outgrow the lust. And although the time had come to start saying goodbye, my love for him would never change.

A few moments later I reopened my eyes and found myself looking at Thomas Hart, who sat across from me, silent and swaying and foaming at the mouth. "Dr. Hart? Are you all right?"

My words didn't register. His eyes remained cloudy and unfocused. Slobber dripped from his chin into his bowl of cioppino. He lurched against the table and then back against his chair, clumsily rising to his feet. He staggered back from the table, upsetting his chair as he wheezed and gasped for air. As he reeled across the floor, Thomas Hart began to collapse. Tossing aside his baskets of sourdough, the chef's helper streaked in just in time to break his fall. Next to reach the fallen scientist was Boyce Reade. "I need water." He bellowed as he lifted Hart's head onto his knees, turning his mouth so the vomit mostly hit the floor. "I need milk. Lots of it."

The chef's helper ran for the kitchen. At Hart's collapse, I'd jumped to my feet, along with Jack McIntire. Only Konstantin Zorich remained seated, but now he, too, rose to his feet, roaring instructions and waving his hand. "Nobody is eating salad! Poison! Please, nobody is eating salad! Deadly poison!"

A groan rose from the assembled guests, and several collapsed into their chairs while flustered companions with shaking hands tried to pour water into their mouths. Lawrence Cameron knelt by one stricken man, dumping water down his throat, while Margaret Armstrong filled glass after glass. Boyce labored at the same task with Thomas Hart, coaxing him to swallow and then making sure he didn't choke when the fluid came right back up.

Konstantin crouched beside my boss, displaying between two fingers a nickel-size slice of vegetable. "*Zygadenus elegans*—Death Camas. Is toxic alkaloid *zygadenine*."

The same plant Cameron had pointed out on our hike to the debris dam! At that news, Jack started pawing through the salads on our table and, after picking through all of those greens, moved on to the next. The chef's helper returned with a plastic jug of milk. I snatched it from his hand and filled a glass for Boyce to empty into Thomas Hart. "Better find some more."

Before taking the glass from my hand, Boyce swept the room with a quick glance and then focused on the Russian. "Go get help. Coppola. And Malloy."

As Konstantin dashed off, I moved through the tent, pouring out the milk, wondering how many of our guests needed hospitalization and how in hell they'd get it. Darkness had fallen, so medevac wasn't even a possibility. And with the bridge out, no one could make the eighty-mile run from park headquarters. Meaning that in this emergency, we were on our own.

I'd just poured out the last of my milk, emptying the jug, when the chef's assistant returned with two more. He handed me one before starting on his own rounds. Dilute, dilute, dilute—that's the first rule of poisoning, and to spare the stomach, often milk is preferred. The technical term is "gastric lavage." But no matter what you call it, the point is the same— flood the stomach with more fluid than can be held. What comes back out carries a lot of the poison with it. And the only poison that gets into the digestive system will be heavily diluted and far less potent.

In the end, only Thomas Hart had swallowed poison potent enough to leave him unconscious. When Ranger Coppola arrived with his stretchers, Hart alone remained prostrate. It turned out that the others who collapsed had sampled the salad and, upon hearing the Russian's warning, jumped to the mistaken conclusion that they, too, had been poisoned. But none of the others foamed at the mouth, lurched out of their chairs, staggered across the floor or dissolved into a vomiting heap. And after a careful inspection of each and every plate of salad or the remains thereof, Jack McIntire determined that only Thomas Hart's salad contained slices of the bulb of a Death Camas. Which meant that his poisoning was no mere mishap. With malice aforethought, someone had doctored his salad with deadly intent.

Even after a medical ranger had stabilized Hart's condition and ordered his stretcher carried to one of the park service buildings, the Wild America mess tent remained in an uproar. I still hadn't told anyone that J. C. Carr claimed to have been pushed, but how she'd been injured wasn't an issue. Arkady Radishchev's death, J. C. Carr's fall and now a poisoning— whether those incidents occurred by chance or design no longer mattered. Three strikes and you're out, and that's just what our conferees wanted—*out!* The scientists milled about the tent, exchanging agitated whispers as Boyce Reade, Ranger Albert Coppola and Special Agent Malloy conferred in one corner. Stray words punctuated the buzz of hushed conversation. Madman. Leave. Impossible. Next.

And when the trio in charge at last shared their conclusions with those assembled in the mess tent, no one seemed satisfied. At this point, the head ranger of Denali Park explained, the only thing anyone actually knew for sure was that the road out of the park would be impassable for at least two more days. Which left us right back where we started, as Jack McIntire pointed out between gulps of Scotch. "Sitting ducks."

CHAPTER 17

TRACKING DALL SHEEP REQUIRES GRIT and tenacity, something Margaret Armstrong certainly had in excess. The stalk also requires the kind of endurance that most sixty-something American women had let slide starting in high school. When we started our quest the next morning at Kantishna's airfield, a frown spread across her lips as Trav loaded our gear. "A tent? Sleeping bags? Are those just precautions?"

Trav ducked out from under the wing and faced her. "Can't shoot on the same day you've flown." He hoisted a sack of groceries from the tarmac. "We'll be spending the night in the bush."

She glanced at me and nodded her gray head toward Trav as he stowed our cache in the plane. "Doesn't seem like much food."

I lifted my shoulders in a shrug, hoping against hope that we could end her hunt right here. "Sheep hunts require short rations since we have to pack out the meat. If you bag a trophy-class ram, that'll only add to the weight we carry down from the high country."

Her eyes drifted away and up to the dark clouds scudding in from the east. After three straight days of clear and sunny, the weather had turned overnight, bringing the nip of autumn to the daylight hours and promising rain. Earlier in camp, we woke to the thrum of propane heaters humming in all the tents, and early risers bundled heavily for their trips to the latrine or mess tent. When I'd offered Margaret an out at breakfast, suggesting that the poisoning of Doubting Thomas called for a reexamination of our priorities, she'd snapped back at me. "Nonsense. The ranger assured us he's recovering nicely." But Margaret Armstrong's hunt looked to be wet and wild, even if we didn't come back with the woolly. Perhaps the prospect of an overnighter would dissuade her. I pressed her again. "We're definitely in for some nasty weather. Are you sure you want to go through with this?"

Squaring her shoulders, she drew herself up to her full height, topping me by a good two inches. "Absolutely! I wouldn't dream of canceling. I've wanted to make this hunt ever since my father left me behind when he came to Alaska when I was a little girl."

I couldn't quite picture her as a child or a daughter or as anyone other than the formidable Margaret Armstrong, Ph.D. Envisioning her with a rifle against her shoulder proved just as difficult. When I said as much, she bristled. "I've been hunting since I was a toddler. Africa, Asia, South America—my father traveled for the State Department and took me everywhere. They called him a diplomat, but he was a sportsman. His job was to hunt with heads of state, and I went along. Everywhere except Alaska."

Looked like trouble—some kind of pilgrimage for *paterfamilias* and not one she'd be easily dissuaded from completing. I murmured something appropriate and ducked under the Piper's wing to help Trav finish packing our gear.

Fifteen minutes later, Trav had us in the air and traveling on a heading south by southeast in the direction of Haines Lake for a gravel-bar landing within the narrow box of land open to aerial hunting just to the west of Denali Park. We'd flown the whole area the day before with Konstantin, peering at the rugged slopes through high-powered binoculars. As the only wild sheep on the planet with white coats, the Dall rams and ewes stood out against the greens and grays of their alpine haunts. Their preference for rocky ridge lines, sheer cliffs and narrow ledges makes every hunt a rough scramble, and even after spotting the quarry by air, actually locating the animals resembles a game of hide and seek. Of course, the trophy-class rams—those whose amber horns have completed the 360-degree circle known as full curl—prefer the most remote slopes, far above the timber line and close to the permanent snow. Unlike many species with solitary males, the Dall rams live in bands which roam the high country in search of choice vegetation, seeking the ewes only during mating season. Of the several bands we'd spotted the day before, Trav had decided to focus on a group of a half-dozen rams which included one spectacular animal that looked to weigh around two hundred pounds. When I pointed out that particular band also lived at the highest elevation, he'd tossed me a wicked grin. "She wants a trophy Dall ram, she'll have to climb for him."

To no one's surprise, Margaret Armstrong proved to be a good hiker. Those sturdy leather boots weren't just for show after all. When we'd finished unpacking the plane at Haines Lake, she gamely shouldered a pack—the smallest, of course, while mine displayed a rather boxy profile—and fell into step behind Trav, swinging along the rough ground with the ease of long practice. She'd probably make it to the top of Denali if she'd a mind to. For the first time since conceiving my scheme to bait-and-switch the older woman, I had my doubts. She sincerely wanted a kill. I sighed deeply and, with a Tibetan brass bell chiming on the frame of my pack to ward off the bears, brought up the rear.

Up or down, rocky or smooth, zig or zag, steep or level, a hike is a climb is a slide is a scramble is an adventure. Sort of. The need to concentrate on my footing and the heart-stopping vistas that opened before us combined to draw my thoughts far away from the troubles back at Wild America's camp. The cloud created by Malloy and her twisted theories evaporated, at least for the time being. The identity of the killer who'd used my automatic to gun down Arkady Radishchev seemed unimportant in this distant locale. The question of why someone would push J. C. Carr from a cliff or poison Thomas Hart's dinner salad faded in importance. As we climbed higher, Boyce Reade's suggestion that I leave Alaska for Washington, D.C., appeared so patently absurd that I had no trouble dismissing it from my mind. Even the ghost of a thought that had nagged at me for twenty-four hours like an incipient headache finally vanished. Instead of letting my mind dwell on my troubles, I concentrated on the physical—the weight of the pack riding against my back and balancing on my hips along with my Smith and Wesson, the strength and elasticity of the muscles of my thighs as my body warmed from exercise and the delicious thrill of a chill thread of air as it lifted the damp tendrils brushing my collar and slid across my hot neck. Back-country Alaska is elemental, which visitors find either terrifying or liberating. Count me among the latter.

Far from roads and dwellings and people, free of the weight of civilization's velvet and grime, my heart and my head lighten, tuned to the rhythm of sunrise and sunset as scored by birdsong, and I find myself renewed.

Two hours into our switchbacking climb, Trav called a break and dug out a tiny stove to make tea. Margaret and I helped each other out of our backpacks and then sat down together, each of us propped against our rig. I split a chocolate bar into threes, tossing one piece to Trav, and offered Margaret first choice of the other two. After a second's hesitation, she chose one and popped it into her mouth. For a few minutes we sat in silence, savoring the chocolate melting on our tongues as the gas stove hissed. Then she surprised me with an unexpected question. "Why did you give up science?"

A glance at her untroubled face told me she hadn't meant to insult me. For many in my profession, any pursuit other than pure research simply isn't science. Some view applied science with scorn. Many prize laboratory work over field work. Most elevate the theoretical disciplines above all others. That chain of respect just doesn't cut it with biology, although cell biology comes close to theoretical science. In my discipline, the problem with theory is ignoring all those living, breathing, mating, eating, birthing and dying critters out there. Biology is, after all, the science of life, and any observant twelve-year-old can tell you that it's hard to reduce life to tidy organized theories.

I swallowed the last smidgen of chocolate, making a big deal of it to cover my delayed response, and finally answered. "Predictions. I gave up research because I hated making predictions. Took all the fun out of it for me."

"Explain." She didn't quite bark the word, but

command rather than request seemed the operative mode, even after she tacked on another word. "Please."

"From the time I was a kid, I loved science, especially biology. I loved learning new stuff, seeing new stuff and finding out how everything fit together." I accepted a plastic mug of tea from Trav, wrapping my fingers around the orange plastic for warmth. As my body cooled with rest, the day's chill penetrated my layers of clothing and raised goose bumps on my skin. "But I discovered at the university that it wasn't enough to make careful observations and draw considered conclusions. Everybody wanted me to predict outcomes, and at each level of academia, the pressure to predict became stronger. Those predictions killed my sense of wonder and discovery, and I just hated it."

Trav hunkered down in front of us. "Sounds like Cameron's complaint about 'Big Science.'"

Margaret Armstrong carefully sipped her blistering tea. "Prediction doesn't have to blind you to the unexpected outcome."

"What's wrong with just letting the experiment unfold?" I tested my tea with my tongue but found it still too hot to drink. "Why not just see what happens and then start theorizing?"

She tilted her head in appraisal. "You're not going to tell me that an intuitive model suits the female scientist, are you?"

"Hah!" Trav rocked back on his heels, splashing tea on the ground. "Not Lauren. 'Physiology is not destiny.' She told me that right off. 'No double standards' is her motto."

I managed a gulp of tea. "Trav's right. I hate all forms of gender stereotyping, including those that claim 'special' abilities in women. But I also don't dismiss Dian Fossey, whose willingness to see gorillas as individuals led to some remarkable insights when all her superiors wanted was a numerical analysis. Or look at Barbara McClintock's work with corn. She told an interviewer that she preferred to work with plants from seedlings so she could get to know them as individuals. Which she said allowed her to get inside the plant, right down there with the chromosomes where she could really see what was going on."

Margaret Armstrong's eyes went a bit dreamy. "For that work she won a Nobel."

I took another gulp of tea. "Bet she'd never have gotten that prize if the guys knew she viewed her plants as individuals and did her best work from the inside!"

About three hours later we reached the heights where we'd spotted the band of Dall rams the day before, an alpine promontory that sloped gradually to higher ground along three parallel ridges. A cold drizzle began to fall midway through our climb, but the roomy ponchos that covered our packs had also kept us dry. The low clouds pressed down from above, leaving stray wisps wrapped like scarves around the higher ground. Trav found a semi-dry spot under an outcropping for our gear and covered the three packs and gun case with a blue plastic tarp tucked tight and weighted with brick-size rocks. After outfitting everyone with a pair of binoculars and a red bandanna, we started the search, each of us moving off on a parallel course across the ridge tops with the reminder that the first to spot game should wave the bandanna in a silent signal.

The patter of rain against my hood replaced the music of my temple bell, but I didn't mind. Not likely to be bears at this elevation, anyway. Pausing every fifteen yards to glass the broken ground above and below me, I worked my way along the ridge, checking every once in a while to see if my companions had spotted anything. A tumble of loose rock that climbers call *scree* to the west looked promising but showed no sign of sheep. A few minutes later a jumble of huge rocks came into view on the east side of the ridge, a pile that looked almost like a cairn except that building it would have required a giant. The powerful binoculars pulled the cairn in close for viewing, but the rock pile was still a good fifteen minute's scramble away. A narrow precipitous bridge led from the top of the pile to a ledge which jutted from higher ground, providing the kind of escape route the wiliest ram would demand. As if to reward my intuition, a slide of loose rock clattered off the huge cairn as a full-curl Dall ram scrambled from one rock to another before disappearing from view. Trophy class!

All right, I'll admit it. For about ten seconds I considered moving on and pretending that I hadn't seen the ram. I could have gotten away with it. No way Trav or Margaret Armstrong could have seen him. But even though I'm certainly not George Washington, I cannot tell a lie, even for a good cause. Shade the truth, maybe. Edit by omission, most definitely. But out-and-out say I didn't see what I actually saw, no way. I pulled the red bandanna out of my jeans pocket and, raising my hand high over head, waved it back and forth, back and forth, until both Trav and our guest responded.

Both had to retrace their steps to our cache before swinging across my ridge top, and Margaret reached me first. Her steps had slowed considerably, but she flashed me a smile before raising her glasses to study the rocks where I'd spotted the ram. Trusting Trav to figure out my signal, I weighted my bandanna with a rock, used a couple of handfuls of stone to fashion a crude arrow pointing to the cairn and led Margaret Armstrong over the rocky ground, taking a circular route to approach the pile of boulders from the front.

A few minutes into our journey, a stiff breeze kicked up, whipping the rain against my poncho and stinging my face. I stopped, grabbing Margaret Armstrong's arm to prevent her from slipping on the loose scree slope. Fatigue etched her forehead, but when I asked if she wanted to turn back, she shook her head emphatically and moved into the lead. A few steps farther and she suddenly stopped, freezing into a stiff unnatural posture.

A single possibility flashed across my mind—heart attack!—before I bolted forward to break her fall.

EXCEPT THAT MARGARET ARMSTRONG
didn't fall. Nor did she move. I charged the distance
between us, screeched to a halt to avoid sending her
sprawling and finally discovered what had stopped
her so suddenly—a robust Dall ram with full-curl
horns whose pristine white wool cast a reverse silhou-
ette against the dark storm clouds. Sheltered from the
rain by a slight overhang, the ram also stood motion-
less, seeming to survey his alpine domain. I held my
breath at the magnificent sight, and for a moment,
Margaret Armstrong did, too. Then, ever so slowly,
she raised her hands to the binoculars hanging around
her neck and lifted the glasses to her eyes, pulling the
ram's image in for an up-close and personal view.

"Watch it! You'll scare him off." The sharp whisper
escaped through the corner of my mouth in a ludi-
crous parody of a gangster à la James Cagney or
Edward G. Robinson. "Vision's their survival sense."

She appeared not to hear me through the driving

rain. Or, if she did, she chose to ignore me and risk spooking her prey for a closer view at his spectacular horns. Although she didn't look to be in the throes of blood lust, I detected a definite increase in intensity. Unresolved kid stuff will do that, as any inner child can tell you. From the sounds of it, the motivation for her hunt stemmed from what? A childhood betrayal? Defection? Abandonment? By her sportsman father. Seeing her on that ridge top standing stiff as an antenna and intent as a coon dog raised a new doubt in my mind. After all, she'd slogged a hell of a ways in abysmal weather to reach this point. If bagging a trophy-class Dall ram meant so much to her, maybe I should do my best to help her. That might be the truly humane action in this situation.

A moment later Trav surfed in on a skitter of stones, balancing in both hands the cardboard box he'd brought me from Anchorage. He flashed me an impish grin before turning his attention to the ram, which hadn't moved at the noise. Perhaps he hadn't heard. Then again, with his visual acuity, sounds could be safely ignored unless he'd already been alerted to danger by movement. Which might mean that since he hadn't seen us, he couldn't hear us. Or perhaps he'd heard, cast us a sideways glance and then dismissed our presence as an intrusion rather than a threat. For Dall sheep, a wolf or a grizzly definitely meant trouble, but a human could often be ignored. We were, after all, trespassers in his kingdom, lowland creatures who'd wandered out of our rightful territory—momentary intruders who might stay a night or two at most but who wouldn't, indeed couldn't, settle in at this elevation. If we had a mind to remain, rain or wind or cold or starvation or winter would drive us back where we belonged soon enough. Over hundreds of thousands of years, evolution had fashioned in Dall sheep an animal perfectly suited to the alpine extremes of altitude and terrain. He belonged, and we did not.

As if sensing my thoughts, Margaret Armstrong dropped her binoculars, swung both arms in a propeller motion and alerted the ram to our presence. "Whoop-whoop-whoop!" Her shout sounded like the Indian war cries of my childhood. In an instant the Dall visibly gathered himself in reaction and then chose flight over fight. A clatter of hooves, a flash of white and he was gone.

Trav let the cardboard box fall to the ground. "What'd you do that for? If you wanted a trophy-class Dall ram, you just lost him."

Peering out of her hooded poncho, Margaret Armstrong eyed the box at our feet and then shrugged. "You said we couldn't hunt and fly on the same day."

He tossed me a sour look that easily pierced the curtain of rain, obviously blaming me for her eccentricity. "Right, I did. But there's no way that guy'll be around to hunt tomorrow."

She raised a serene face to him and smiled. "And neither will we. What's in the box?"

I scooped up the soggy cardboard and held it out to her. "Something I asked Trav to pick up for you in Anchorage."

Her eyes lit with Christmas-morning joy, and she wrenched open the box with the eagerness of a child to reveal white acrylic fuzz and amber felt. "What on earth——" She lifted the stuffed ram's head from the box and turned to me open-mouthed and wide-eyed.

"I was going ask you to imagine the living ram's eyes replaced with this guy's glass." My turn to shrug. "Looks like you made the connection without my help."

She clutched the stuffed ram against her chest. "I'm no altruist. I could have had that ram if I'd wanted him. At my age, oftentimes knowing that is enough.

Especially when you run out of time." She rubbed her cheek against artificial fleece beaded with water and sighed. "I am grateful not to be leaving empty-handed, Lauren, and will treasure this memento of a spectacular day. But now I'm afraid it's time to go back."

Hiking down to the plane was not part of the day's plans, despite the wishes of my guest and Trav's client. Not that I'd been looking forward to spending the rest of the day mummied inside a down sleeping bag stuffed in a pint-size tent, the only rational camp activity in light of the day's ceaseless drenching. Given my druthers, I'd have preferred the long slippery slide back to Haines Lake. But I'd scared myself silly with that heart-attack scenario and didn't want to be blamed for the untimely death of Margaret Armstrong. I sincerely didn't think she had the stamina to make it up and down in the same day. When sputtering and fuming at her proved unpersuasive, I tried to enlist Trav in my cause. "Tell her she's nuts, MacDonald. Tell her that lots of times going down is worse than climbing up."

All the way back to our cache, he'd listened to our exchanges in silence, the crushed cardboard box tucked under one arm while his free hand steadied Margaret Armstrong. After settling her out of the rain, he'd quickly cooked up a couple of envelopes of noodle soup and dug pilot bread, dried fruit and Vienna sausages out of our pantry pack. At my plea, he set aside his steaming mug and faced me squarely. "I'd trust Dr. Armstrong's judgment on this one. She didn't get where she is by being careless. Besides, sounds like she's got a damned good reason for getting back tonight."

With that last bit, he didn't even have to add "ungrateful wretch" to get his point across. Turned out that the chief beneficiary of returning today would be me since Margaret Armstrong's "damned good reason" consisted of stepping in to co-chair tomorrow's review of Soviet research that the late Arkady Radishchev originally had been scheduled to lead. Despite his death, J.C.'s fall and Hart's poisoning, Wild America's conference had proceeded as planned, at least for the healthy guests. If, however, Margaret Armstrong didn't return to camp today, a major glitch would occur. Meaning that, with the overall success of the venture hanging in the balance, I'd have to be a fool or worse to continue with my objections. And so with all the good grace that I could muster, I conceded the wisdom of her plan, gamely shouldered my now less-boxy pack and tried to content myself with the tinkle of the brass temple bell at the rear of the line.

Our sodden trek down from the high country was the exact opposite of the morning's ascent. Low clouds rolled in, hugging the ground in a disorienting fog, and rain pounded down in waves that battered the heavy PVC of my poncho, drowning the soothing sounds of the bell. The tinny drumming set my teeth on edge. After stubbing a toe of my hiking boot on a protruding rock, I slalomed across the slick tundra vegetation, precariously balanced on one foot, until another rock sat me down hard just as Margaret Armstrong's forest-green poncho disappeared in the fog ahead. Longing to blubber like a child, I had no choice but to get back on my feet fast or risk losing my companions. Taking the time to feel sorry for myself could wind up placing me in mortal danger. Instead I scrambled to my feet, ignoring both bruised ego and posterior, and trotted back to my spot at the rear of our little expedition. Neither Margaret nor Travis had noticed my absence. And so the journey continued, one foot in front of the other with a few breaks for rest, until late afternoon when we finally reached

Trav's plane on the gravel bar at Haines Lake. No sooner had we taken off than the rain stopped. Naturally.

Margaret snored in the co-pilot's seat the whole way back to Kantishna while Trav concentrated on his gauges, his radio and "this damned squirrely weather," leaving me to stew over the great unpleasantness which awaited me back at Wild America's camp at Wonder Lake. In the shadowed corners of the Piper's cabin lurked wraiths which represented Malloy's crackpot theories, the killer hiding among us and Boyce's suggested move to D.C., all ready to swoop down to smother the day's pleasure with their unremitting bleakness.

To shut them out, I closed my eyes and pressed the *play* button on the mental videotape labeled Konstantin, fast-forwarding through my fresh memories and hitting *pause* when an image appeared that I wanted to linger over—the tremble in his strong hands when he told me about his wife during our midnight picnic on the banks of the McKinley river, the enthusiasm in his green eyes when he described the breathing of trees, the swiftness of the decision that sent him down a treacherous slope to rescue J. C. Carr. And among those images came one which froze on its own, a vision of Trav and Konstantin and me flying high over Denali's glaciers as the soundtrack played my own voice in a continuous loop: ". . . a pharmaceutical firm provided funding so they could run tests on a new drug . . . a pharmaceutical firm provided funding so they could run tests on a new drug . . . a pharmaceutical firm provided funding so they could run tests on a new drug . . ." The insight armed me for battle with the shadowy wraiths, but first I needed to enlist the Russian on my team.

Back on the ground at Kantishna's airfield, Trav MacDonald bid us a hasty goodbye. With darkness coming on and worse storms in the forecast, he needed to skedaddle if he wanted to get back to Anchorage that night. Since Margaret Armstrong had forgone the wilderness layover, his job was finished, although he offered to stay. "Getting socked in with a bunch of Ph.D.s doesn't sound too appealing, but I suppose I could manage. Just in case."

"Just in case what? The little lady needs some assistance?" I forced myself to grin and patted the revolver as I slipped the holstered gun into the top of my backpack, safely out of sight but handy enough for comfort. "You already brought in the cavalry." When I got back to camp, I'd need to devise a better rig for the weapon. "I'll be fine."

He considered the heavy clouds scudding across the sky, studying those surging in from the east with special care, and then turned back to me. "If you're sure you'll be okay."

I heaved a sigh. "What did they teach us in flight school? 'From a high to a low, watch out below?'" I jerked a thumb toward the east. "That does not look good, Trav." Reaching up on my toes, I brushed a quick kiss across one cheek. "I'll be okay. And if you leave now, you will be, too."

I'll admit that my heart tightened a little when, after one climbing swoop around Kantishna's airfield, his Cessna steadied on a course carrying him away from Wonder Lake. Good friends can be hard to find when you get to the sticky places in life, and at that moment, I knew most definitely that Wild America's Gaia conference could be classified as a true quagmire. But even with Trav gone, I wasn't alone. More than once since I'd met him, Konstantin Zorich had demonstrated courage and compassion, and I was betting loyalty was another part of the mix. With his best friend the first victim, the fight was his more than Trav's. And Konstantin's friendship with Radishchev and his knowledge of science provided him with the tools that we'd need to build a trap for the killer hiding among us.

Darkness gathered along the edges of the gravel road as I prodded Margaret Armstrong into a faster pace. Too caught up in fevered speculation to spare anxiety for any grizzlies in the vicinity, I shouldered my pack and even carried the stuffed ram, folding it against my chest as I slowly but steadily increased my speed. She trotted beside me without complaint, yawning a bit and seeming unwilling to break the silence. After skirting the stumps at the fire ring, I'd intended to detour to the Russian's tent, leaving Margaret Armstrong to continue on alone to the one we shared on the other side of camp, but neither of us got past the ugly mob milling outside the mess tent.

Perhaps *mob* is too strong a word. As Margaret and I entered the circle of tents, all eyes fell upon us. In fact, I had the distinct impression that all hands were actually waiting for us. I scanned the faces, looking for my new friend, but didn't spot Konstantin Zorich, Lawrence Cameron or Boyce Reade. Jack McIntire stood to one side of the tent's screened doorway, alternating drags on a cigarette and gulps from the glass in his other hand. Arrayed around him were about half of our guests, most clutching glasses liberally filled with Wild America's happy-hour offerings. And standing before them, apparently the only one without a cocktail of some sort, was a pale-faced Thomas Hart. Before I could ask how he was feeling, Doubting Thomas tossed a question to me. "Where's the pilot?"

"Gone." Crushing the stuffed ram's head with one arm, I flapped the other like a wing. "Back to Anchorage. There's a huge storm coming in, and he didn't want to spend the next few days here, stuck on the ground."

A soft moan swept the circle of scientists, and Hart stepped toward me. "That was his plane we just heard? You mean, you actually let him go?"

I glanced at Jack, but his eyes slid away, so I focused on my prosecutor. "What's wrong with that?"

"We're trapped. That's what's wrong." Thomas Hart bristled with equal measures of animosity and fear. "Trapped with a murderer." An edge of hysteria lent a quaver to his voice. "He's already killed once and tried to make me his second victim. And I don't care what anyone says. It's murder, I tell you!"

Once again, I found all eyes upon me: Jack McIntire's narrowing with speculation, Thomas Hart's glittering with unshed tears and Margaret Armstrong's widening with apprehension—an apprehension shared by the others gathered outside the mess tent. They seemed to be waiting for me to deny Hart's words, but I didn't. It was definitely murder, and I could now say that with confidence because I knew the motive. And from the *why*, I would discover the *who*. Eventually. So I didn't say anything. Not just yet. Not until I could also say who.

CHAPTER

19

I THINK I KNOW WHAT'S GOING ON here." At my words, Konstantin tilted his head with interest. I'd felt a little funny slipping into his tent after dinner, but appearances be damned. I needed his help to get from *why* to *who*. "I think I know what the killer is after."

In his chair alongside the campaign table at the front of the tent, the Russian leaned toward me in invitation, propping his elbows on his knees. "Tell me."

"Why did Arkady Radishchev come to this conference? Because he was a devotee of Cameron's Gaia theory?" I crossed my hands on my lap to keep them from trembling. "No! He came for one reason—to lead a review of Soviet biological research to rescue any findings that might have been shelved for political reasons. Is that right?"

Konstantin gave me a firm nod. "Correct."

"Arkady Radishchev came to lead a review, but he never got the chance. Someone killed him. We've been wondering why, but we've overlooked the simplest, most obvious reason for someone to kill Arkady Radishchev." From my seat at the foot of the late scientist's cot, I leaned toward the Russian, basking in the stream of hot air blown from the propane heater at the foot of the cots. "I think he was killed to stop him from leading that review."

For a long moment Konstantin said nothing. The gas lantern hissed behind him on the desk, joining the thrum of the heater to provide a steady undercurrent to the muted chirruping insects in the sodden woods beyond the circle of tents. I leaned toward the Russian while he leaned toward me, but no further confidences were exchanged. Instead Konstantin pulled back inside himself, his eyes fixed in an unseeing stare as his mind retreated to weigh my words. Finally his gaze refocused on my face. "And what of Hart? This poisoning?"

I flashed him my grimmest smile. "Not just Hart. J. C. Carr told me someone pushed her off that cliff."

The Russian's eyes widened and then, very quickly, narrowed into a sharply pointed stare. "Pushed? And you are not telling me?"

A shrug underscored my apology. "Sorry, but back then I figured she was delirious. Now I think she was pushed for the same reason Arkady Radishchev was killed. And Hart poisoned. To stop tomorrow's review."

Another long stare and then he sat back in his chair, sighing deeply. "But why?"

I raised a hand. "Before I go any further, I need to ask you a couple of things." I paused to choose my words carefully. "You told me about Lysenko and some of the problems with science in Soviet days. What if one of your scientists discovered something really important? Something that could stop cancer, say, or something to regenerate severed nerves?

Would the Soviets have ignored that kind of discovery?"

At my last question, he laughed, a bitter chuckle that seared me. And then he answered. *"Nyet."*

At his denial, my heart plummeted, but before I could sit back, he leaned forward and grabbed my hands. "Lauren, Lauren. The problem with Soviet system is not coming from evil men. The problem is coming from stupid men. And stupid scientists. No, Soviets are not ignoring discoveries." He gave my hands a gentle squeeze. "But perhaps stupid scientist is not seeing discovery." Another quick squeeze. "So now you are telling me why is someone killing Arkady to stop Soviet review."

Forty years of Cold War blather had left the Russian with as much ignorance about American capitalism as I'd just shown about Soviet communism. Americans take for granted the notion that every question boils down to one overriding consideration—the almighty buck and how to make some. Without the benefit of familiarity with either our consumer culture or the myriad ways Americans have devised to cash in, Konstantin simply didn't have a clue. I walked him through my scenario twice, then he talked himself through it a third time, just to make sure he had the concepts down. "You are saying someone is killing Arkady to stop review."

At my nod, he continued. "You are saying in review someone has found important discovery."

Again I nodded, and again he continued. "You are saying this discovery is probably pharmaceutical."

I had to jump in. "I'm guessing about what the discovery is, Konstantin, but I do know that more than forty percent of all drugs—that's what we call pharmaceuticals—derive from living things. For instance, taxol, a revolutionary cancer drug that comes from yew trees, and epibatidine, a painkiller two hundred times more powerful than morphine that derives from South American frogs."

To emphasize my point, I slowed my words. "Both of those drugs are incredible breakthroughs. Taxol stops cell division, meaning it stops cancer. And epibatidine works on receptors in the brain that nobody even knew existed."

Konstantin rocked back in his chair, balancing on the rear legs. "Yes, yes, yes. This much I am understanding. But why is someone stopping review? Why is someone keeping this discovery a secret still?"

"Okay. Here it is." I leaned toward him, speaking slowly and clearly. "Pharmaceutical breakthroughs generate big money. A successful cancer drug can earn a billion dollars a year. And these days, the scientist who does the basic research gets a piece of the action. Meaning some new drugs are literally worth millions of dollars, maybe hundreds of millions, to the discoverer."

I sat back and spread my hands. "In this country, money is often a motive for murder." The line from P. D. James echoed in my mind. "And the greatest of these is lucre." The drug/money scenario worked for me, but Konstantin still looked doubtful. "There's something in that research that can be turned into money. Lots and lots of money. That's why I believe the person who reviewed the Soviet research and found the overlooked discovery is also the person who killed Arkady Radishchev. Someday soon the killer will pass off the breakthrough as his original research and reap the reward."

After I finished, the Russian again retreated behind his eyes as he weighed my words. Finally, but oh-so-slowly, he nodded. "And you are saying that the poisoning of Thomas Hart and the pushing of J. C. Carr is also to prevent this review?"

I let out a sigh of relief. He'd gotten it. "I think so. I

think the killer keeps trying to get the damned review canceled. But maybe J.C. really was delirious. And I suppose Hart's poisoning could have been some kind of accident." Another, grimmer thought crossed my mind. "Or, he might have poisoned himself. As a distraction. If Hart's the one."

That gave us both something new to think about, taking us to the heart of the problem—*who?*—and we both fell silent. As we'd talked, the camp outside Konstantin's tent had gradually quieted. The clatter of pans in the kitchen subsided first. For a while the door of the latrine had banged open and closed, open and closed, as gas lanterns glowed through tent walls and propane heaters growled to life across the camp. But, one by one, the lanterns had winked off, and the heaters had fallen silent. Now even the insects had stopped chorusing. Only a hooting owl and the steady drip from the drenched trees filled our human silence.

"Aarrgghh!"

A scream ripped through the hushed camp.

"No. NO! *NO!*" The scream dwindled to a sobbing moan. "Oh, God, he's killing me!"

The screamer's panic galvanized Konstantin. He leaped from his chair and answered the cry. "All must rise now!"

His roar raised the hair on my neck as he vaulted toward the screen door. "All must come now!"

The feeble light escaping a clouded moon outlined his shape as he flung open the screen and disappeared out the door, still roaring a rallying cry and leaving me to scramble to the floor in search of my pack and my gun. I burrowed one hand into the pack until my fingertips brushed cool metal. Flip and snap, I'd checked the ammunition in the Smith and Wesson. Then I followed him out of the tent to face an unknown danger in the darkened camp.

"Konstantin!" My voice rang hollow in my ears. "Where are you?"

"Here! At your tent. Come quickly. She is hurt."

A half-dozen beams of light sliced the dripping darkness, darting wildly from the doors of as many tents. I ran in the direction of the one I shared with Margaret Armstrong, ignoring the shouts erupting around me, the revolver tightly gripped and hanging at my side. Sprinting the length of the camp took mere seconds. I arrived in time to experience a disorienting moment of *déjà vu* as Konstantin Zorich lifted Margaret Armstrong through the shredded side of our tent and knelt on the ground, cradling her across his knees in a horrific rerun of our first meeting three days earlier. Before I could drop to my knees to complete the replay, a scuffle behind me sounded an interior alarm and I spun, raising and bracing the .38 until the barrel pinned in place the new threat.

"Jesus, Lauren, don't shoot!" Boyce Reade carried a high-powered flashlight in one hand and a first-aid kit in the other. He had the good sense not to blind me with his light and to ask my permission before moving. "Let me help her, for God's sake!"

I nodded, too shaken to speak, and lowered the revolver until the barrel pointed at the ground. My heart thumped a brutal tattoo inside my chest as he slid by me and knelt beside Konstantin. I'd been ready to kill him. No lie. I had been ready to pull the trigger on my boss. Not that I was eager to shoot him, mind you. Far from it. But I had been prepared to shoot Boyce Reade, which of course was the whole point of the rigorous training regimen that I'd followed all summer. A cop friend told me that if I wanted to carry a gun, I'd better learn how to use it so I'd be prepared when the time came. I had, and I was. And now a sickening little worm of certainty uncoiling in the pit of my stomach told me that my actually pulling that trigger was just a matter of time.

"Not too deep, thank God." Boyce played the beam of his flashlight over the wound in Margaret Armstrong's arm, dabbing at the well of blood with a gauze pad, while Konstantin held her steady. "Are you hurt anywhere else?"

"No. Nowhere else." She tried to lift herself. "Thank you"—the effort proved too much, and her head lolled back against the Russian's shoulder—"for coming."

One of the chef's helpers appeared, casting away the darkness with the lantern he carried, and I realized he'd been the one who came running with the first-aid kit when Konstantin discovered Arkady Radishchev's body. His eyes darted from the trio kneeling in the mud to the darkness over his shoulder. "Crowd coming."

"We can use that lantern. And your help." I moved next to him, making sure he saw my gun as I spun the cylinder to an empty chamber before jamming it inside the waistband of my jeans and fluffing my fleece pullover to hide the bulge. Then I held out my hand for the lantern. "Think you could run over to the park service camp and roust the FBI?"

After another glance at the tableau before him, he nodded his agreement and disappeared into the night. As a light drizzle began to fall, I placed the lantern beside Boyce and picked up his discarded flashlight, then moved to shoo the mini-mob of gaping bystanders who appeared out of the darkness to lurk just at the edge of the pool of lantern light. "She's okay, guys."

A sudden gust of wind that also carried a shower of rain flickered the flame of the lantern, threatening a full and wet darkness, but the conferees made no move to disperse. Walking forward with both hands held up like a traffic cop, I tried to redirect the herd. "Don't know yet what happened, but Margaret's okay. Got a slice on her arm, but she's talking while they fix her up."

I clicked on the flashlight, panning the crowd with a brilliant cone of light as their voices rose in speculation—a discordant, unhappy chorus. At the back edge of the crowd, Lawrence Cameron fussed, trying to advance but unable to break through. By his elbow stood Jack McIntire, bleary-eyed and disheveled from sleep.

"Move aside for Dr. Cameron, folks." I gave my grad school pal the high sign. "Jack, help him get through, would you?"

Leading with one raised hand, Jack plowed through the herd, bumping aside shoulders and elbows as needed. Behind him came Lawrence Cameron, threading through the same opening, to add a fourth penitent kneeling in the lantern's pool of light. Across that tableau, Konstantin Zorich met my eyes, raising his eyebrows slightly before giving me a solemn nod. The attack on Margaret Armstrong confirmed that we were on the right track. She was scheduled to co-chair the review of Soviet research. Somehow we had to make sure the other chair, Lawrence Cameron, lived through the night. And maybe, if we had time, we'd conduct a review of our own. After all, if the killer had found something important, so could we.

When Special Agent Malloy showed up a few minutes later, trailing a sizable pack of park service employees, including Head Ranger Albert Coppola, the shower had turned into a steady rain, but none of the gaping guests had moved back to their tents. A worried murmur containing only a few distinct words buzzed over the crowd. *Danger. Attack. Madman. Again.*

Their behavior reminded me of a story Max told of

the night in Montana when a grizzly dragged a woman out of her tent in an isolated trailside camp. After the other campers rescued the mauled woman, they stayed together, huddling in the light, to wait out the darkness. And so the Gaia conferees huddled at the edge of the light, ignoring the steady rain, finding safety in numbers against the predator who stalked from inside our human circle. Across our huddled mass, a wave of relief relaxed stiff shoulders and tight faces when Malloy and Coppola appeared in our midst.

The FBI agent bristled with authority, raising her voice and all but brandishing the 9mm in the shoulder holster strapped outside her sweats. "Ranger Coppola, I want your men spread out as a perimeter guard. Starting right now, no one enters or leaves this camp without my say-so."

For the rest of the night, I felt a bit like the little goat in *Jurassic Park* that finds itself tethered inside the cage of Tyrannosaurus Rex. Not that I hadn't ever found myself in more immediate danger. I had, and recently. Just three months earlier, I'd faced down a charging grizzly. Soon after, I'd dodged bullets fired from a marauding helicopter. And then I'd survived a drowning scare when my boat was intentionally sunk in the frigid Yukon River. But in those three incidents, the danger—while harrowing—arrived unexpectedly. One moment the trail stretched empty before me and the next a grizzly pounded down it. One moment the helicopter flew peacefully and the next it spat lead. One moment the boat skimmed over the water and the next dived under the surface. A few minutes of absolute terror I could handle. The slow inexorable buildup of tension and threat was something else.

More than once in the course of the long night I spent in Konstantin's tent, my hand slipped under the bulky sweater I'd borrowed from the Russian to fondle the body-warmed handle of my Smith and Wesson. After much trial and error in converting my hip holster to a concealed body mount, I wound up looping the belt over my shoulder and under my arm, guerrilla style, with the holster jutting across my belly and secured in place by the tie-downs snugged through a belt loop. After tugging Konstantin's sweater back over my head and settling it around my hips, I stretched this way and that, getting a feel for the new rig. Not only could I breathe and get quick access to the revolver, but my effort at concealing the gun seemed to be successful. Neither the park service prohibition of firearms nor the threat of provoking Special Agent Malloy fazed me. With a killer on the loose, my .38-caliber equalizer offered welcome reassurance. After months of dedicated practice, I definitely knew how to use the weapon. And as I'd proved to myself earlier that night when I sighted in on my boss, I could use it without hesitation if I had to.

Only one minor glitch threatened our plan to pull an all-nighter to sift through the Soviet documents in search of the research that someone had decided was worth killing for. We spent a good hour futilely searching for the necessary paperwork, beginning with the belongings of Arkady Radishchev before moving on to the shredded tent I'd shared with Margaret Armstrong.

"Nothing!" After slapping my tent mate's canvas carry-on in irritation, I rocked back on my heels. "Nearly empty now, but it was stuffed before, literally jammed with papers, slides, computer diskettes! I ought to know. I've been tripping over the damned thing all weekend!"

"And not tripping am I!" Konstantin closed his eyes and tilted his head. "As we are coming here, I am carrying two bags. And Arkady? From shoulder is hanging one—for under his bed. And in his hand is hanging another? Yes!" His eyes opened, and he stomped a heel on the carpeted floor. "Yes, another! I, too, am tripping in the darkness. Then I am moving bag to table."

My heart clonged at that news. "The table in your tent was empty, Konstantin. When we went back after finding Arkady Radishchev's body, the table was bare."

"Correct. So with Margaret Armstrong's empty bag is coming Arkady's lost bag. All for stopping our review." His lips curved into a grim smile. "Now to Dr. Cameron?"

Lawrence Cameron had insisted on accompanying his wounded colleague when Malloy ordered Margaret Armstrong moved to the park service camp, but our search of his empty tent turned up nothing. So why did this triple disaster only result in a minor glitch? Just as I opened my mouth to admit defeat, the Russian rode to the rescue. "I am giving thanks for bad Russian transport systems." He took my hand and gave my fingers a reassuring squeeze. "I, too, am carrying these papers."

With one smooth movement, he raised my hand to lift me from the floor. "Come, Lauren. We must be reading and reading and reading. The answer is hiding in those papers, and we must be finding it."

Not it, him. And what it all came down to was him or us. But I didn't say that out loud. Neither of us needed a reminder that lives were at stake. When the Tyrannosaurus Rex moves in your direction, stark raving terror doesn't let you forget.

Konstantin's hoard of paperwork for the review of Soviet research made a couple of impressive piles on the campaign table in his tent. Mostly summaries of experiments that dated from as early as the 1950s, the findings had been translated into English before smaller packets had been made up and shipped off to individual conferees for analysis. Just gearing up for the review had required a lot of work on somebody's part. "Who did the translations?"

"Each laboratory is selecting own translator." Konstantin shuffled one stack of papers, neatly lining up the edges. "At my laboratory Arkady is translating."

"But he didn't speak English!" Despite the surprised widening of Konstantin's eyes, I distinctly remembered Malloy telling me that Radishchev spoke no English. When someone accuses you of murder, all those little details tend to stand out. Radishchev's inability to speak English had provided the plot line for one of the FBI agent's scenarios that starred me as the killer. Your basic miscommunication gone ballistic. "Special Agent Malloy said that Arkady Radishchev didn't speak English."

"A police? And you are believing her?" He shook his head at the utter naiveté of anyone who believed what a cop told them. "Arkady was having excellent English—reading, writing and speaking."

Suckered! A surge of anger left my cheeks burning and my hands shaking. The FBI agent had played me for a fool with her fantasy scenarios built on a foundation of phony facts. But why?

"Now we are starting." Konstantin handed over a sheaf of papers two inches thick and shifted in preparation for leaving his chair. "For you the desk."

"No, you stay there." I carried the papers over to Arkady Radishchev's cot and stretched out. "This is the way I worked when I was in college. That's the last time I was really any good at this stuff."

The steady rain had eased back to a shower that pattered gently against the canvas of the tent. In the camp outside, an uneasy quiet had fallen, the sodden drip occasionally pierced by restless sighs, hushed whispers and muffled coughs. For a while the only sound inside came from turning pages. After scanning a couple of dozen, I realized that not a single word had registered in my brain. My fatigue and irritation at Malloy's trickery had blinded me to the meaning. I allowed myself three deep cleansing breaths and then asked for clarification. "Konstantin, what exactly are we looking for? I mean, how do you spot stupidity?"

He swung around in his chair and gazed at me over the top of his reading glasses, looking rather adorably professorial—a thought I firmly pushed away. "Perhaps promising direction is being ignored. Perhaps method is flawed. Perhaps conclusion is not being justified."

Perhaps I was way out of my league. My aversion to prediction and mathematical models had led me to abandon pure science years before. Given my recent credentials, my place in applied science might better be termed a toehold than a foothold. My preference for field work and passion for advocacy made me somewhat of a renegade in wildlife biology. And what lay stacked before me was botany, reams and reams of chemical and structural analyses of plants.

Classical botany starts with a series of division and classification questions. Bryophyta or Tracheophyta—does the plant have plumbing? That's the first division. Filicinae, does the plant reproduce with spores; or gymnospermae, does the plant reproduce with seeds; or angiospermae, does the plant reproduce through flowers? That's the classification. Such basics represented the level of sophistication of the right-off-the-top-of-my-head botany that I brought to the task at hand. Meaning not much.

I snuck a glance at Konstantin, who bent over his papers, worrying his lower lip with his teeth as his hand alternated between tracing the course of his reading down a page and sliding the glasses back to the bridge of his nose. I might be a bit rusty on my science, but at least the summaries were written in my native tongue. Konstantin had the disadvantage of translating from an English translation back to the original Russian before weighing the promise, methodology or conclusion of each report. Not that you had to be a cutting-edge researcher or a fluent bilingualist to understand the bottom-line principle involved.

Bottom line, what we were looking for was a discovery that could prove useful to humans. When you're studying plants, usefulness almost always comes as food or medicine. And in the race to translate usefulness into dollars, medicine beats food any day. Fewer than three percent of the planet's known angiosperms, or flowering plants, have been screened for medical utility. So what? Consider the rosy periwinkle of Madagascar, which produces pretty five-petaled blossoms and two powerful alkaloids —vinblastine and vincristine. Most people suffering Hodgkin's disease or acute lymphoctic leukemia have heard of the plant because the rosy periwinkle saved their lives. Survival in the first disease went from two percent to fifty-eight percent and in the second from twenty percent to eighty percent when the plant's alkaloids entered the battle against those deadly cancers. With that kind of success, the drugs' annual earnings reach into the hundreds of millions of dollars. Imagine a three-percent royalty from that discovery!

For a moment I studied the findings of a chemical analysis performed by fast atom bombardment mass spectrometry on *Porphyra laciniata,* the lacy green seaweed the Tlingets call "Thalkush." The Soviets discovered the plant to be rich in iodine, the element essential to the proper function of the thyroid in humans. Like so many other health-promoting plants, the usefulness of *Porphyra* was long understood by natives. In fact, careful study of folk medicine might be a good way to identify potentially useful plants. That's how Western medicine came up with quinine as a treatment for malaria and curare as a muscle relaxant. Already twenty-five percent of American drugs derive from plant extracts, and the National Cancer Institute has identified three thousand plants that contain anti-cancer agents. Current research indicates that as many as ten percent of the Earth's plants may contain compounds that can battle cancer. Why do plants contain such chemical weapons? Researchers theorize that plants may produce alkaloids to protect against disease or insect attack. Other metabolites may poison predators, and produce odors and colors that attract pollinators. The Earth's present flora represents the natural wisdom of 450 million years of evolution. In comparison, homo sapiens has stalked the planet for only two hundred thousand years. Is it really a surprise to discover that your average Sitka Spruce might know something that has thus far escaped the mind of man?

Such were my thoughts as I poured over the summaries of Soviet research, sifting for overlooked promise, flawed methodology, unjustified conclusions or some other imperfection that represented the difference between the mundane and a miracle. As we worked, a great weight descended on my eyelids, much too much weight to resist. And so without putting up any fight, I allowed my head to slip lower and lower until at last my cheek found a pillow on the dwindling stack of Soviet summaries. One tiny flickering region of my mind hoped that Konstantin wouldn't be too disappointed in me. The far larger portion descending into a blessed darkness simply didn't care.

C H A P T E R

21

THE FIRST TIME I WOKE, I DISCOVERED that Konstantin had replaced my stack of Soviet summaries with a soft pillow and snuggled a warm fleece sleeping-bag liner around me. I opened my eyes as a cool moist breeze swept through the mosquito net window just inches from my face. The rain had stopped, but water still dripped from the trees overhead. No light showed in the camp beyond, and the silence in the tent left me wondering if Konstantin had left? Just then he sighed and turned a page. And so, knowing he was near, I let my eyes close again.

The second time I woke, I rolled onto my back. The propane heater near the door growled, the oil lamp on the desk flickered and Konstantin still bent over his papers, his search fueled by a box of crackers at his elbow. I levered myself up from the cot. "Find anything?"

He turned to me with a smile. "No. Not yet." He lifted the box of crackers. "Hungry?"

"No." The effort of raising myself had finished me.

174

I barely got the word out before flopping back onto the pillow and sinking back into slumber.

The third time I woke, the pink streaks of sunrise tinted the clouds that streamed like flags flown from the icy peaks of the distant mountains. No light showed inside the tent, but in the pink dusk of dawn, I made out Konstantin on the opposite bunk. He'd slipped into his sleeping bag and lay on his back, arms propped beneath his head.

I reached across the space between us and touched his elbow. "Did you find it?"

He rolled onto his side and faced me. "Yes."

My heart leaped, and my voice was little more than an excited squeak. "Who is it?"

He gave me a tired smile. "I do not know."

I shook my head, my mind still dulled from sleep. "I don't understand."

He raised a hand to smooth a dark curl from his eyes. "Who is doing review I do not know. I find summary, not killer."

I pulled the fleece liner up to my chin. "Tell me."

"Is Arkady's own work from many years ago. He is screening plants for cancer medicines." He sighed again, a sigh of despair as much as exhaustion. "Now he is reviewing his own work. And someone else also, of course. For this he is killed."

I burrowed deeper into the fleece liner, warding off a shiver born more of fear than cold. "You mean he sent his own work off for review? And also reviewed it himself?"

"Yes." How bleak one word can sound.

"Tell me about his research."

"When Arkady is coming to Siberia, little is known of plants there. Of minerals, yes. Of animals, yes. Fishes to eat, seals for skins—of such resources much is known." He shifted inside his sleeping bag. "But of plants, nothing. Even of timber, little. For peoples needing wood, Siberia is too far."

He rolled onto his back, offering me his face in profile. "And so my friend is beginning his study. Plant by plant, he is cataloging all species. Year after year, plant after plant, until each is being named, each is being examined. This is his work of forty years. The work of his life."

I nodded, but Konstantin didn't see. Instead he stared up at the canvas ceiling of his tent. "And somewhere in that early research he overlooked something?"

The Russian smiled then—a crooked, trembling smile. "Arkady is missing nothing. Such dedication. So thorough he is."

"I don't understand." My frustration leaked into my voice. My turn to sigh. "I'm confused. If Arkady Radishchev missed nothing back then, what's the problem now?"

"Back then, for culturing, everybody uses cells of mouse. Arkady as well." Konstantin turned his head to me. "Now more is being known. Today using mouse culture is no more. For today, we are screening with human cells."

"You mean the chemical screening was faulty?" My mind zoomed on ahead, but my mouth took it step by step. "So everything screened back then against cells cultured from mice should now be screened again against cells cultured from humans?"

He nodded. "Correct. So, Arkady is doing again his screen, and his killer as well. And now both are finding something. Faulty culture was making faulty research. Many times was this true with cells of mouse."

"Tell me about it. All of our diet drinks got pulled when lab rats developed bladder cancer from dosages equivalent to a human drinking a hundred gallons a day." I went up on one elbow. "What plant are we talking about?"

"Alnus rubra." He gave me a tired smile. "The alder."

Hardly an exotic or even rare species, the alder grows profusely in Alaska, too, creating impenetrable thickets in poor soil along rivers and roads. Who would have cast such an ordinary plant as a hero in the battle against cancer? "So in all of those summaries, only the methodology of the alder research is faulty? No promise overlooked? No unjustified conclusion."

"No and no." He shook his head firmly at each no. "Only is alder faulty. Only alder shows promise against cancer."

My mouth finally caught up with my mind. "So, what do we do? How do we connect Arkady's research to his killer?"

He rolled his head on his pillow, staring up at the ceiling of the tent and speaking very slowly. "At review, we are listening. When is coming alder, does reviewer talk of mouse cells?" His forehead furrowed. "If yes, I am wrong. If no, is reviewer hiding promising research and are we finding the killer?"

That evidence seemed too flimsy to support a charge of murder, and I said so. "Maybe the reviewer just spaced? What if he just overlooked that detail?"

Konstantin's eyes glittered in the silvering light of dawn. "My friend, Arkady, is dead. And then is coming J. C. Carr's fall and Thomas Hart's poison and Margaret Armstrong's knife. This killer is overlooking nothing."

When I didn't reply, his eyelids fluttered and then closed. Looked like the lack of sleep was taking its toll. By my guestimate, almost two hours remained before breakfast, leaving the Russian time for some shut-eye and me time for some thinking. We'd moved on to a waiting game, needing only to fill the hours until the moment arrived for the killer to reveal himself. We will know him by his review. Wait until the subject is alder and then listen carefully. When the reviewer fails to mention faulty methodology due to the use of mouse cells, we'd have both the confirmation of motive and the identity of the killer.

Outside the tent, the squeak of bedsprings, rustle of sleeping bags and buzzsaw snorts of restless human slumber punctuated a subdued installment of the camp's morning chorus of birdsong and squirrel chatter. The overnight rain had left the air sodden and heavy, seeming to dampen the critters' usual A.M. cheerfulness. One part of me wanted to rush right over to the park service camp to let Malloy know that we'd figured things out, and she should be ready to cuff the perp. Another part of me pictured her response—curled lip, haughty chin, amused eyes and a voice that dripped with scorn: "Mice? You're saying this is all about mice?" That was all the provocation I needed to get mad at her all over again. After all, she had lied to me about Arkady Radishchev's knowledge of English. Which proved how much she liked nasty little games, ones I had no intention of playing anymore. I unpeeled myself from the fleece blanket snugged around my shoulders. And who cared how she'd take that news?

Coppola's park service crew still manned the perimeter of Wild America's encampment, but a shift change provided the escort I needed to penetrate their line. At the park service complex, I found Albert Coppola alone in the bunkhouse where I'd had my "interview" with Special Agent Malloy. She'd turned the place into living quarters as well as an office. A ratty old easy chair stood near the propane heater, and one of the cots had been made up into a bed. The rest of the frames and mattresses had been piled at the far end of the cabin, and a rickety card table with a couple of battered chairs had joined the two desks at the end nearest the door. Denali Park's head ranger sat at the card table, one hand holding a pot of coffee and the other brandishing an empty mug. He nodded toward the chair beside him as he poured out the dark brew. "Cream? Sugar?" After setting the mug in front of me, he tempted me with a plate of fried cakes fresh from the oil. "Now you can't say that the federal government's never done anything for you."

After wolfing down one fried cake, I managed to proceed a bit more decorously with the second by forcing myself to swallow, pause and ask a question between each bite. "How's Margaret Armstrong?"

"Pretty shaken up." He selected another fried cake. "She calmed down once I let another of your scientists into her cabin. Fellow named Cameron."

Swallow. Pause. "What happened, anyway?"

"Hard to tell because she was asleep when it started." He tore the fried cake in two and dunked one half into his mug of coffee. "Looks like the knife wasn't all that sharp. Poked through the canvas okay, but in the end, the attacker had to rip the tent. That's what woke her."

"Sharp enough to cut." I blew across the top of my mug of steaming coffee. "Sharp enough to kill."

Coppola nodded. "If it had connected. As it is, she'll have a jagged scar but not much else. Bruises will heal."

Swallow. Pause. "Did he say anything? I mean, if it was a man?"

"It was a man, all right. At least from her description. Big. Looming. Strong." The ranger dunked the other fried cake half into his mug. "He didn't speak, but he grunted like a man. That's what she said. Also said he stank like a man. And he smelled of whiskey."

That narrowed the suspects to the half of our

conferees who'd drained a bottle of Jack Daniel's, Chivas Regal and Wild Turkey each night since the conference began. Boyce couldn't believe the liquor consumption of our guests, confessing he'd expected scientists to be a bit more abstemious. Unfortunately, Margaret Armstrong proved to be among the few teetotalers in attendance and couldn't identify the booze scent any more definitively than whiskey, which drew a big sigh from Special Agent Malloy as she returned to the bunkhouse. "Not much to go on, I'm afraid."

I literally had to nip the end of my tongue with my teeth to keep myself from asking her the question which instantly sprang to mind: Since when had lack of evidence stopped her from making an accusation? Talk about bitter! I'll admit it. At that moment I was very bitter, with a shriveled heart thumping in my chest and a shrill voice squawking in my head. For reasons I couldn't fathom, Special Agent Malloy had toyed with me about Arkady Radishchev's murder. Now that I knew how to identify the real killer, I could admit the absurdity of my fear of her string of implausible scenarios featuring me as a murderer. Hindsight's like that, after all. Unfortunately, foresight's another problem entirely. I knew, of course, that I should tell the FBI agent the conclusions Konstantin and I had reached and devote all the hours that remained before the review, if necessary, to making her understand the significance of those damned mouse cultures. Knowing what should be done is easy. Actually doing it is hard. And sometimes impossible. Before I could bring myself to risk Malloy's curled lip and scornful voice, I wanted the answer to one simple question. And so, after finishing my second fried cake, I cleared my throat to get her attention, and when those green eyes turned in my direction, I lobbed her the query. "Why did you lie to me about Arkady Radishchev's language ability? He spoke fluent English."

I stared at her as I waited, trying to skewer her with my eyes, but she refused to look away. Or to answer. The seconds must have stretched into minutes, and still she remained silent. Finally, thankfully, her shoulders lifted into the tiniest of shrugs. Then she rose from her chair and stalked from the bunkhouse, all without a word. And somehow her silence stung me more than spoken scorn ever could.

CHAPTER

22

Our killer's passion for details almost cost Konstantin Zorich his life later that morning. When I returned to Wild America's circle of tents, a chill wind blew splatters of rain across the soggy camp. At breakfast the conferees gulped cup after cup of steaming coffee, arming themselves against the damp with a caffeine boost that further ratcheted up the tension level. As I trickled cream over my oatmeal with blueberries, Boyce took the podium microphone to inform our guests that the temporary bridge had been completed, opening the Denali Park road to bus traffic once again.

"Since most of Wild America's guests expected to be here until midafternoon anyway, the park service has given priority to regular tourists." When a groan went up from those assembled, Boyce played his trump card. "In light of Arkady Radishchev's death, completing the review seems the least we can do."

Across the table, Konstantin Zorich raised an eyebrow, but Boyce didn't notice as he returned to his seat. Nor did he notice when I slipped my hand under the bulky Russian sweater for a swift brush of reassurance over the warm smooth metal of the Smith and Wesson .38 snugged against my belly. A woman with a gun might be every man's worst nightmare, but, after all, a nightmare is just a bad dream. And as I'd told my kids countless times, dreams can't hurt you because dreams aren't real. Of course, after their first dose of Sigmund Freud, that line will no longer work. Nightmares can become reality in a heartbeat, but in the welcome light of a new day, such a reversal seemed unlikely.

Following Boyce's announcement, a wave of giddiness swept the mess tent, born of the utter relief many felt at having survived the night, the last night they'd spend trapped with a killer. By dinner, every one of us would be back in Anchorage, and by noon tomorrow, most conferees would be on their way home to the Lower 48. And if all went as Konstantin and I had hurriedly planned in his tent just before the mess bell summoned us to breakfast, Special Agent Malloy would soon be feeling her own brand of relief. We'd agreed on a simple course of action. When Arkady Radishchev's killer revealed himself, the Russian and I would simply pass the name on to the FBI, explain the reasoning behind our accusation and let the feds take it from there. My kind of plan—simple and safe.

As the cleanup crew cleared away breakfast, Thomas Hart did his best to scuttle the review, insisting that the public process was an empty exercise that would be more efficiently handled by telephone, fax, E-mail or snail-mail. Ordinarily, I would have agreed with him. The format did seem a bit like the dreaded orals in graduate school—each reviewer taking the podium to describe his findings on specific Soviet research and then answering any questions from the assembled scientists. And, in fact, Konstantin admitted to me privately that Arkady Radishchev had rigged the public process with that end in mind. As the man designated by the new Russian government to oversee fat contracts for scientific consultants, he'd devised the public process to review the reviewers. Nobody else knew that. And nobody else knew that Arkady Radishchev's death insured that the public process was anything but an empty exercise, offering what might be our only chance to identify his killer.

While we waited for the cleanup crews to complete their tasks, freeing the mess tent for the review, most of our guests poured another cup of coffee from the fresh pots placed on each table and remained in their seats, some probably due to elementary good manners and others probably due to wicked hangovers. Doubting Thomas provided the single exception, stalking off in extreme high dudgeon and leading me to entertain the notion that he might be our killer, one clever enough to avoid suspicion by poisoning himself.

The first hour of the review session added weight to my notion. As the minutes ticked past and the Soviet research under review did not include *Alnus rubra,* the alder, I actually began to hope. Scientist after scientist rose from his seat, carried a sheaf of papers to the podium, detailed his review of Soviet analyses of as many as three plants and answered a smattering of questions. How the murderer might have managed to kill Arkady Radishchev at Wonder Lake and then arrive on the shuttle bus from park headquarters that afternoon didn't interest me. At that moment I preferred answers, even easy ones. No sign of Thomas Hart *and* no mention of alders? Hah! Eventually, I became so caught up in the notion, marveling over such serendipity—Doubting Thomas! Of course!—

that I made the mistake which almost took Konstantin's life. When a reviewer finally spoke the taxonomic classification of alder, I gasped.

At the sound of my distress, my grad school pal Jack McIntire hesitated almost imperceptibly before detailing the findings from his review of the Soviet research into the structural and chemical analysis of *Alnus rubra*, findings which did not include any mention of the use of cell cultures derived from mouse tumors, fake findings that overlooked a promising new avenue for cancer research. And because he was a good lab rat, Jack McIntire would have noticed the faulty screen done with mouse cells, and he would have redone the screen using human cells. Because, as Konstantin had said, Arkady Radishchev's killer overlooked nothing. As he returned to his seat after completing his presentation, the full horror of the killer's identity finally hit me.

Jack. My ears filled with the rushing silence that deafens me when I'm truly shocked.

Jack? My stomach clenched in a painful contraction that left me sickened and weak.

Jack! I wanted to vomit and to scream and to run to some faraway place where old friends always remain incapable of cold-blooded murder.

Could he have spaced the mouse culture? Could he have overlooked such a minor detail? No. Not Jack. Lots of people, maybe, but not Jack McIntire. Stray memories from our days at Cal echoed in my ears. 'A demon on details!' 'Talk about finesse—the guy's a magnet for nuance.' 'I think I've got a problem figured out, and then McIntire walks in to show me all the subtle stuff that makes it so much more complex.' In my experience, Jack McIntire never overlooked any detail, however minor. And that morning in the mess tent, my pal proved he hadn't lost that edge. When

Lawrence Cameron called a break a few minutes later and I dragged Konstantin outside into the drizzle for a hasty consultation, Jack followed us.

After leading the Russian under the sheltering branches of a spruce beside the mess tent, I turned to face him just as Jack slipped his arm around Konstantin's shoulders and pressed an eight-inch blade against his throat. "You figured it out."

A simple assertion, stated flatly and without emotion. At the sharp kiss of the knife against his throat, Konstantin had stiffened, and now he remained silent. I couldn't. "Jack—"

"Shut up, Lauren. And start walking." He loosened his grip, sliding a hand until it latched on to Konstantin's arm, and then used that lever to steer the Russian deeper into the woods while keeping the sharp blade pressed against his flesh.

I fell back ahead of them, my hips and shoulders clutched by shrubbery as I backed into the dripping shadows. "Jack, this is crazy. You can't escape. There's no way out."

"Sure there is. There's a road." A smile flickered across his lips. "And a bus."

Konstantin's eyes remained calm, but he moved slowly and stiffly, like a wooden doll. When he stumbled over a gnarled root, Jack caught him, surprisingly strong for a man who had seemed pretty flabby. Still the knife bit into Konstantin's throat, drawing blood which seeped over the bright metal blade.

The sight froze me. "Jack, stop! He's cut!"

An ugly smirk twisted his lips, and he tightened his elbow against Konstantin, who gave a little grunt of pain. "Then he better watch his step."

I had an urge to run, to dart away into the shadows, rip the gun from the belt hidden under my sweater and then take Jack from behind, but he anticipated me. "Don't try anything, Lauren. If you run, the commie's history." His flat voice, his dull eyes and the blood dribbling on Konstantin's neck heightened the menace of his words.

And so I floundered on through the forest, face scratched by unseen branches that whipped back against my cheeks, afraid to turn my back on Jack, needing to maintain eye contact with Konstantin. Had they missed us? Had Boyce come looking for us? Had anyone seen us leave? Did Jack plan to kill us, figuring that no one would find us for hours or days or weeks? Of course, he couldn't kill us both because I had the .38 and knew how to use it. But as soon as I went for the revolver, Jack would kill Konstantin. One firm slash and the wound would be mortal. Suddenly, knowing how to use the Smith and Wesson wasn't enough. *When* became the only consideration. Timing was everything.

"Stop right there!" Jack hissed the words. "Don't move." Shoving Konstantin ahead of him, he came up beside me, careful to keep his knife arm away from me. "There's the bus. Count the passengers, and find out when they're leaving. Then signal me."

I glanced over my shoulder. The yellow school bus idled at the shuttle stop, about ten yards down the road.

"Go on, Lauren." He jiggled the knife at Konstantin's throat, smearing the blood against his collar. "Go check it out."

Drawing only deep cleansing breaths to maintain my cool, I stepped out of the woods and strolled toward the bus. As I walked the length of it, I glanced at the windows, hoping to find lots of grinning tourists but coming up empty. Not a single passenger. The long-haired kid who'd ferried us close to the Muldrow Glacier sat behind the wheel. I tried to make my smile genuine. "When are you leaving?"

"Another couple of minutes." He glanced at his watch. "Yeah, just under five."

I attempted to inject a bright note into my voice. "No passengers? What gives?"

"Couple of buses already left—both jammed." He shrugged. "Maybe you docs are the only ones left."

Moving off a few steps, I turned to face the woods where Jack waited for my signal. After miming a turning wheel, I raised one finger indicating the presence of the driver. After miming the bouncing of a seated passenger, I circled my thumb and fingers into a crude zero, meaning no passengers on board. And after pointing to my watch, I held up four fingers, meaning four minutes until departure. Before I lowered my hand, Jack steered Konstantin out of the woods, and they walked with twin jerking movements toward the bus, the knife still firmly pressed against Konstantin's throat.

I kept hoping the long-hair would glance in his side-view mirror, spot the knife and then stomp on the gas, gunning the bus out of there. I didn't dare draw the revolver. I didn't dare whisper a warning, not with Jack staring me down. Helpless to act, confidence withering, I came close to breaking. Until my eyes drifted to meet Konstantin's level gaze, and his calm eyes restored me, speaking without words. Patience, *krasavista.* You must have patience. His thoughts echoed in my mind.

Jack motioned me to the other side of the open bus door and then swung into the driver's view with a snarl. "Outta the bus, kid, or this guy dies."

Wide-eyed and gape-mouthed, the long-hair slowly raised both hands in surrender and eased up from the seat.

"Come on, move it." Jack kicked the bottom step as the kid sidled toward the ground. "Lauren, take the wheel. And you"—I scrambled into the bus, but at

Jack's growl, the driver froze—"have them call me on the radio. Get my demands."

Shoving Konstantin ahead of him, Jack climbed into the bus, breathing heavy now. However strong, he carried too much weight for any of this to be easy. Red-faced and sweating, he forced Konstantin into the first seat of the opposite aisle and then dropped into the seat behind him, knife still pressed against the Russian's throat. "Get this bus moving."

I threw up my hands. "I don't know how to drive it."

The knife bit into Konstantin's throat, drawing fresh blood. "Figure it out."

AFTER SHOVING THE STICK INTO GEAR,
I eased out the clutch, and with two ominous bounces,
the bus rolled forward, spitting gravel and dust behind it. Checking the side-view mirror, I spotted the
long-hair running out of the choking cloud of dust
and in the direction of the camp at Wonder Lake.
He'd get help. Not that anybody could do much about
Jack McIntire when he had a knife pressed against
Konstantin's throat. A sniper with a scope, maybe,
but that seemed unlikely with both hunting and
firearms prohibited inside Denali Park. Which made
me a million times happier that I'd chosen to break
the law—again. I had the means to end the standoff; I
just needed the opportunity. And when I got my
chance, I wouldn't blow it.

As the engine whine reached an excruciating pitch,
I punched in the clutch and yanked down the stick,
hoping to find second gear. The bus continued
smoothly down the gravel road, picking up speed and
enough momentum to carry us over the little hill that

rose ahead of us. I tossed a glance over my shoulder, meeting Jack's rigid stare. "Alder, huh? So how good is it?"

He sat behind Konstantin, left hand clamped firmly on the Russian's shoulder and right hand maintaining the pressure of the knife against his neck. The Russian slouched against the bench seat, his eyes counseling patience. "Beyond my wildest dreams." A pothole jounced us. "Watch the road."

Risking his anger—wanting it, really, so he'd make a mistake—I used the rearview mirror to search out his gaze again as I shifted into third. "How does it work?"

"Cytotoxity—the stuff actually kills the cancer cells." His glance flicked up to meet my eyes in the mirror and then dropped. "The cell starts to divide but can't. So, eventually, the cell dies."

He lifted a hand from the Russian's shoulder and pointed at the dashboard. "Flip that radio on and off a couple of times. See if it works."

Gripping the wheel tightly with one hand, I leaned to my right, reaching for the knob that controlled the CB radio, and spun it on and then off, on and then off. With each spin of the knob, a crackle of static cut in and cut out. "Seems to be working. Maybe the driver got lost in the woods." Shift into fourth. Another glance in the mirror. "Maybe he ran into a bear."

No reaction from Jack McIntire. Maybe bears didn't scare him. The road ahead angled toward the north in a slow descent, falling toward the river that had washed out the bridge. Would the construction crew still be on site? Would Jack recognize the scenery and ask himself the same question? Just in case, to distract him, I threw out another question. "So what do you figure your discovery is worth?"

"Radishchev's discovery, not mine." At that admission, Konstantin stiffened, and Jack McIntire patted his shoulder. "Hey, I don't mind admitting it, fella." Was that a little catch in his voice? "Even admitted it to him, for all the good he got out of it. He could have had millions."

My left foot hovered over the brake, and I eased the wheel into a turn as the descent steepened. "Millions?"

"That's right—millions." A heartbreaking chord rang in Jack's voice, a curious mixture of longing and awe and regret. "I've got a deal worked out with a biotech lab in San Jose, a start-up firm looking for a quick winner to underwrite more speculative genetic work. Ten million bucks for all rights, including the patent. Radishchev could have had half."

For the first time Konstantin spoke. "Half? For his own work, the work of his life, you are offering him half?"

The Russian's sudden sharp intake of breath drew my eyes back to the rearview mirror. Fresh blood welled at a nick just under his left ear, a nick just over his carotid artery. "Why not? Why shouldn't I get a finder's fee? After all, he fucked up the original research, and I was the one who discovered that!" Jack's mouth twisted in a snarl as he thrust his face forward to confront Konstantin, half rising from his seat. "Fair's fair, buddy—he had to share credit, but your pal didn't want to. Not that he wanted the money, either. 'Our gift to the world,' he said. 'Yeah right' I said. 'What planet are you from?'"

After a quick survey of the road ahead, I stared into the mirror, willing the Russian to meet my eyes and understand the message they contained. Don't provoke a guy holding a knife at your throat. Let me provoke him, so he'll let down his guard with you! As quickly as Jack's anger flared, the rage also subsided, and he sat back down.

The bus rounded a final curve, revealing a narrow makeshift bridge of plywood, lumber and stout spruce, freshly cut and still bearing bark. The workmen had left a portable outhouse and a small trash barrel overflowing with crushed cans and stray wrappers, but except for a crisscross of muddy ruts, the parking area lay empty.

Releasing a silent sigh, I downshifted into third and took the one-lane bridge at around thirty-five miles an hour, the bus thunk-thunking over the uneven surface before reaching the welcoming crunch of the gravel beyond. After downshifting to second for the climb out, I risked another glance in the mirror and found Jack McIntire's brooding eyes staring up the drainage toward the lake that was no more. "Did you push J. C. Carr?"

For a moment he didn't answer. Then he turned his head to face the road again, his eyes bleak and his voice a hollow gust. "Yeah, I pushed her."

The left front wheel bounced through another pothole, but he didn't seem to notice. I pulled the bus back to the center of the gravel road. "And Thomas Hart? Did you doctor his salad with Death Camas?"

He didn't reply, so I risked another look over my shoulder and found him nodding silently while outrage tightened the Russian's face into a mask of fury. "Not his—anybody's. I didn't care who choked down the Death Camas. I just wanted out." He shook his head, lip curled in disgust. "I wondered, 'Shit! What does it take to get this shindig canceled?' Your boss must be a fucking Brit with that stiff-upper-lip crap. Even after I knifed Margaret Armstrong, he wanted to carry on."

Before I could respond, his voice turned bitter and self-mocking. "And then, after all of that effort, Doubting Thomas starts his crybaby whining this morning and almost pulls it off." With one whipsaw movement, he gave Konstantin Zorich's shoulder a sharp slap. "Too bad you stayed out of it, fella. One word from you and the Soviet review would have been history." Jack's voice sharpened again. "But you kept quiet, comrade, and now you're paying the price."

"And I'm paying double, right, Jack?" Keeping my eyes from the rearview mirror took all the strength I possessed, leaving my voice without energy, flat and matter-of-fact. "First you shoot Arkady Radishchev with my gun and try to frame me for the killing. Now you're making me the wheel man in this asinine attempt to escape. You're such a pal, Jack. That's what friends are for, right?"

Without warning, the radio squawked to life, a stuttering of static with words unintelligible. I reached for the CB mike, but Jack McIntire stopped me with a word. "No. Leave it. You'll call them when I'm ready and not before."

Again the radio screeched, and again I badgered him. "So what's your plan, Jack? What are your demands? You going to ask for a plane, Jack? Get your ten million in ransom? Play this like an action movie? No offense, Jack, but you're not my idea of a leading man for any kind of Arnold art."

"Shut up and drive, Lauren." His hand moved to the Russian's head, fingers twining through dark curls. Then he yanked Konstantin's head back, baring his bloody throat, and pressed the knife against the torn flesh. "Just shut up and drive."

And so I drove, heading toward what I remembered would be a slight rise followed by a longer curving grade with the bank falling away on one side and a steep slope looming on the other. Anticipating increased velocity when the bus started down the grade,

I got ready to shift gears again but topped the rise only to find the road ahead blocked by a brown bear sow and her twin cubs. After stepping off the gas pedal, I eased in the clutch and started to brake, praying the damned bus wouldn't fishtail on the gravel road.

"Why are you stopping?" Jack craned around Konstantin's head, trying to see. "Don't stop."

"There are three grizzlies blocking the road." Slowing, slowing, holding steady, almost stopped. "I can't get around them."

"Then get them out of the way." Jack roared as he yanked Konstantin off his bench, dragging him forward toward the driver's seat. "Give them the horn."

As the bus finally halted with a small jerk, he let down his guard, dropping his steering arm to reach for the horn on the wheel and simultaneously releasing the pressure on Konstantin's throat. When Jack leaned away from the Russian, Konstantin made his move, a vicious backward jab of the elbow that speared Jack in the gut. The force of the blow drove both of his arms forward. He managed to keep the knife but lost his hostage when Konstantin dove out the folding door. And when Jack regained his composure, he found himself staring down the barrel of the Smith and Wesson .38-caliber revolver braced in my hands.

"You won't shoot me, Lauren." He brandished the knife, blade freshly stained with the Russian's blood, and started to reach for the gun. "We've been friends for too long."

Jack McIntire got it half right. We *had* been friends for too long. I'd maintained my loyalty to him long after he'd betrayed my trust. My pal had used my own gun to kill a man and tried to pin the blame on me. Not a very friendly act. And certainly not an action deserving a second chance. The night before I'd realized that the time was coming when I would actually pull the trigger with malice aforethought. Looked like that time had just arrived.

As his knife neared my jaw, I aimed at his widest spot and squeezed the trigger. The shot caught Jack McIntire in the gut, spreading a red blossom and knocking him through the bus door.

CHAPTER
24

AFTER KONSTANTIN ZORICH AND JACK McIntire flew out the door of the bus, the grizzlies needed no more persuasion to scramble up the steep slope on the opposite side of the road. I had the presence of mind to grab the microphone of the CB radio and call for help. "This is Lauren Maxwell in the shuttle bus. We need medevac ASAP."

A bit of static, a brief cacophony of voices and then the reply. "Say again?"

I took a deep cleansing breath. "This is Lauren Maxwell calling from the bus. We need immediate medical assistance."

More static and then the voice of authority. "Maxwell, this is Special Agent Malloy. What's the status of Professor McIntire?"

I glanced through the open door of the bus. Konstantin had rolled Jack onto his back and spread a clean pressed handkerchief over the wound in his gut, and now the Russian's hanky glistened red. "Not good. He may be dead before you get here."

More static and more words, but I didn't listen to her reply. I simply waited for a pause and then spoke again, not trying to be funny, just trying to let them know I was through talking. "Signing off. Over and out." I let the microphone fall from my hand and climbed down from the bus to see exactly what I had done to my old grad-school pal.

Jack McIntire lay on his back with eyes half closed, face paling to white and chest moving with shallow jagged breaths. Konstantin knelt beside him, clasping one of Jack's hands between his own. Bright slick blood pooled around his knees.

"They're coming." I took the other side and the other hand, kneeling in the gravel. "I wish they'd hurry and get here already."

Sometimes wishes do come true. It turned out that when the long-haired bus driver showed up at Wonder Lake, insisting that hostages had been taken, Chief Ranger Albert Coppola had summoned the rescue helicopter under contract to Denali National Park. And when I called in from the shuttle bus, requesting medical assistance, he simply redirected the chopper to our presumed location, informing the pilot of a medical emergency. Within minutes of my wish, the helicopter appeared, buffeting us with rotor wind as it settled to the ground about fifteen yards down the road. With stunning efficiency, the crew lifted Jack McIntire onto a stretcher, loaded him into the chopper and whisked him away. So much for the illusion of wilderness in the Great Land's most famous national park. When Special Agent Malloy arrived a few minutes later, the only remaining sign of Arkady Radishchev's killer dripped from the knees of Konstantin's blood-soaked pants and puddled on the wet road. She looked from the Russian to the pooling blood to me. "What went on here?"

Grabbing the .38 from the holster still snugged to

my belly, I handed her the revolver and then walked away, heading back up the road toward Wonder Lake and leaving Konstantin to answer her question. After all, he was the eyewitness. I was the shooter.

People always claim to feel numb at moments like that, and it's true. I did feel numb. Meaning I felt nothing in the same weird way you feel nothing when a dentist pumps you full of Novocaine. Your mouth still works, but your tongue seems thick and your lips seem fat and you feel nothing. As I walked over the slight rise on my way to Wonder Lake, my body still worked, but my legs seemed heavy and my arms seemed flabby and I felt nothing. Only a matter of time till I actually pulled the trigger, and now that time had come and gone. I'd pulled the trigger and shot a man. Not just any man—my friend. And maybe not just shot. Maybe killed. And I felt nothing.

Warned of Malloy's approach by the scuff of feet against the gravel road, I kept walking. "Mrs. Maxwell." She fell into step beside me, a shimmer of moisture on her brow but breathing steady. "We'll need to talk about this."

I didn't miss a step. "Not now."

She hesitated for a moment and then jogged forward to catch up with me. "Okay. I've got the gun. That's all I really need now. And the Russian. I'll take his statement." She kept pace beside me. "You probably want to get back to town. See your kids. We can talk later."

Still marching, still numb. "Fine. I'll give you a call in a couple of days."

Lots of callers tried to get through in the next few days, but my kids and my house mate threw up a net that snagged them all. Taking turns as phone and door monitors, Jake and Jessie and Nina Alexeyev simultaneously kept the word at bay and spun a protective cocoon around me that assured unlimited rest when I wanted sleep and unlimited pampering when I awoke. Mostly, I slept, sometimes the heavy and unmoving sleep of exhaustion and sometimes the light and fretful sleep of anxiety. In between, my son and daughter and best friend babied me with comfort food and comfort music, pampering me like a cherished invalid. All three seemed to understand just what I wanted and just what I needed. And so, on the day that I woke, finally wanting and needing someone else, I found myself absolutely unsurprised when Konstantin Zorich appeared at my bedroom door, breakfast tray in hand. "I am making Russian tea. Best in the world."

As I drank sweet tea from the glass in true Russian fashion, he told me that in the days of my oblivion, Jack McIntire hadn't died and in fact was now out of danger. Welcome news, to be sure. Not that I felt anything. Still numb, legs heavy and arms flabby, I didn't feel anything when, with the Russian by my side, I finally called Special Agent Malloy. He stayed with me on the outing that highlighted my return to "normal." First stop, the Federal Building in downtown Anchorage.

Malloy emerged from the inner office to greet us. Konstantin protested when she explained that he couldn't possibly be allowed to overhear my statement, but I managed to reassure him that I'd be okay. For a little while I thought he might make a real scene, so great was his distrust of any police, but in the end he accepted my decision, promising to remain on alert in the waiting room and respond immediately if I called for assistance.

Once we'd managed to alleviate the Russian's suspicions, Malloy led me down a short corridor to a small conference room where three men waited. Names escaped me but titles stuck. The sandy-haired fellow with tortoise-shell glasses was an assistant United States Attorney, and the other two—dressed in identical blue suits, although one wore a red tie and the other a striped tie—were FBI agents. The lineup didn't faze me. So numb was I that if J. Edgar Hoover *and* Efrem Zimbalist, Jr., had walked into that conference room, I wouldn't have broken a sweat. What a difference a week makes.

Malloy motioned me into a chair on the opposite side of the table from the trio of men, creating a face-off across the long side, and then selected for herself a chair at one of the short ends of the table, staking out the middle ground and apparently not taking sides. The FBI agent with the red tie took the lead in questioning me, covering the usual ground, talking me through the tumultuous weekend at Denali National Park day by day, looping back now and then to clarify chronology and refine cause-and-effect. No, I didn't inform my boss or park authorities or Special Agent Malloy that I had a weapon in my possession. No, I didn't want to explain how the Smith and Wesson came to be inside a national park. Yes, Konstantin and I had agreed on a plan for identifying Arkady Radishchev's killer via the review session. No, I never considered sharing Konstantin's identification of the alder summary with Special Agent Malloy. Yes, providing the killer's identity seemed to make more sense than trying to explain to a non-scientist why a particular research summary might be significant. Who expected to be taken hostage like that, in the middle of the crowd that managed to completely miss the main event? Yes, Jack McIntire's identity made sense in a twisted, angry-white-male way. Yes, money. Absolutely, he was a truly gifted teacher, which counted for zilch in an age when most people considered practitioners of that profession to be suckers. Bitter ain't the half of it. Yes, I did consider it self-defense. No regrets. Remorse, maybe, but no regrets. Right, I was certainly no pacifist and also no martyr.

My lack of regret and refusal of martyrdom obviously bugged the assistant United States Attorney. When the red-tied FBI agent pressed those points with me, a flush stained the prosecutor's cheeks, color deepening with each flat unemotional answer that I gave. Finally he could stand no more. After silencing the fed with a dismissive wave of his hand, he sat forward, scowling at me through his tortoise-shell glasses. "Your interpretation of the facts of this case is unimportant, Mrs. Maxwell. The only opinion that counts is that of the federal grand jury that will hear the evidence and hand up indictments. And that grand jury is going to want to know why you willfully violated, on two separate occasions, the federal law that prohibits the possession of firearms within a national park, and exactly how the second firearm came into your possession. I expect that how you choose to answer those questions, and when, will have great bearing on whether or not the federal grand jury hearing the evidence concludes that you wounded Professor McIntire in self-defense."

The threat implicit in his words managed to penetrate the numbness that had deadened my reactions for days. But before I could bestir myself to answer in kind, Special Agent Malloy jumped into the fray. "Oh, come off it, Gil." She pushed her chair back from the table and sprang to her feet. "That kind of badgering is abusive, and you know it." She stalked toward me, taking up a position behind my chair. "As soon as we ID'd McIntire's fingerprints on the diskettes that we dug out of the Wonder Lake latrines, we had all the evidence we needed to confirm the version of events described to us first by Konstantin Zorich and now by Lauren Maxwell." Her hand dropped to my shoulder. "If you want to ask questions, fine. But consider yourself notified that if you continue to abuse this witness, I intend to file a formal complaint."

To a man, the trio on the opposite side of the table shared mirror reactions—eyes narrowing, jaws clamping and shoulders stiffening. For a long moment no one said anything. Then the prosecutor flashed a quick smile, sly and thin like a reptile's grin. "Well, well, well. Colleen Malloy shows her true colors at last." He dug a money clip out of his pants pocket and peeled a twenty off a thin wad, placing it on the table in front of the agent with the striped tie. "You called this one right, Jake. Looks like she really is a feminazi."

Not until the prosecutor used her first name did I realize that, to me, the woman with her hand on my shoulder had been simply "Malloy," another one-word label as dehumanizing as the insult just flung in her face. Colleen. I wouldn't have guessed that in a million years.

Colleen Malloy's hand slid from my shoulder to my upper arm, fingers circling in a gentle grip that urged me to my feet. "Time to go, Mrs. Maxwell. I think we've both heard more than enough."

CHAPTER 25

AFTER COLLECTING KONSTANTIN ZOR-
ich from the waiting room, Colleen Malloy marched
me down a dingy staircase, through the lobby of the
Federal Building and onto the sidewalk beyond. Finally, with Seventh Avenue's man-made mountains of
concrete and steel looming around us, she paused long
enough for me to ask her a question. "What was that
about Jack's fingerprints on a diskette found in the
latrine?"

She studied the blank windows of the Federal
Building before answering. Then her gaze dropped to
meet my own, her green eyes open and free from
calculation for the first time since we'd met three days
before. "After your conference cleared out, we took
that campground apart. All of Margaret Armstrong's
missing files—including those on paper and those on
computer disks—turned up in the sewage under one
of the latrines. The forensics guys were able to recover
quite a few clear prints from Professor McIntire."

Konstantin chimed in with a question. "And files of

Arkady and Lawrence Cameron? You are finding those also?"

Colleen sighed and shook her head. "Nope. No sign of those yet. But what we have should be enough to nail him for Radishchev's murder."

"But how did he manage it?" I squinted my eyes against the afternoon sun, conjuring up the memory of death in the early morning as passersby streamed past, some with the determined stride of the workaday world and others with the relaxed stroll of the leisure set. "How did he get to Wonder Lake without anyone seeing him? I can understand how he took my gun without waking me up, but what about the shooting itself? Even I couldn't sleep through the bark of that .45, and yet I did. Has he said anything about how he pulled that off?"

The last question prompted a snort of disbelief from Colleen Malloy. "Once the doctors let us in to talk to him, he asked for a lawyer. First thing, 'I want a lawyer.' And after getting one, McIntire hasn't said anything else. And most likely won't."

The Russian seemed genuinely impressed by the notion that an accused man could refuse to answer questions, but that didn't stop him from tossing in a few of his own. "But still you are thinking of these questions, Colleen Malloy, of how and what and why? And you are finding answers?"

"How and what and why?" She tilted her head and her eyes went distant. "I think Jack McIntire came to Wonder Lake the same way you did, Mr. Zorich—on foot. I think he wanted to get to Radishchev before the conference opened and make his deal—a fifty-fifty split of ten million dollars. While you were sleeping, your friend took a walk and McIntire followed, introducing himself and outlining the deal. Only problem was, Radishchev turned him down."

I nodded vigorously. "We know that's true. Jack

said as much on the bus. So that's when he took my gun?"

Returning my nod, she drew us out of the sidewalk traffic and into the lee of the Federal Building, hard by the solid wall. "Right. I don't think he planned to kill Radishchev. I don't think it ever occurred to him that the Russian would turn down five million dollars. Maybe McIntire went looking for you, his old friend, to pour out his tale of woe. And maybe he just happened to see the Colt on your desk. That, I think, is when he decided to lose his unwilling partner. Pure impulse, and for the first time in a very methodical life, he gave in to it, with disastrous consequences. And what better place for giving in to impulse than in the middle of the wilderness?"

My turn to tilt my head as I considered her observation. "Are you saying that the wilderness itself somehow inspired Jack to kill?"

She lifted her shoulders into a shrug. "Maybe. Look at it this way. As far as we can tell, this guy played by the rules all of his life. Then, for the first time, he goes to the wilderness, not the woods but true wilderness. A place with a whole new set of rules—predator or prey, kill or be killed—rules that require quick, almost impulsive decisions."

The Russian leaned a shoulder against the bulk of the Federal Building. "With impulse, he is killing Arkady. With impulse, he is pushing J. C. Carr. With impulse, he is poisoning Thomas Hart. With impulse, he is knifing Margaret Armstrong."

Colleen Malloy had answered most of the hows. Although I considered pressing her on a procedural point, asking her to speculate on how Jack McIntire managed to fire my Colt .45 automatic without rousing the entire camp, I remembered what a cop friend had told me about the inevitable loose ends in any murder investigation. Besides, I had a more important question for her. "How come you rode to my rescue in there?" I jerked a thumb at the Federal Building. "A couple of days ago I asked you a simple question, and you walked away without bothering to answer. This afternoon you're a different person entirely, more like Joan of Arc."

To my utter amazement, her eyes instantly filled with tears and she whispered one simple word. "Shame." She blinked rapidly a couple of times. "Shame on both counts."

She glanced at the Russian with a trembling smile and then back to me. "You'd asked me why I lied about Radishchev's language ability, and I walked out because I was too ashamed to tell you the truth. I lied about that for the same reason I hit you with those phony accusations—to jerk you around, shake you up. Because I'm with the FBI and that's the way we operate, with the emphasis on macho adversarial bullshit."

She took a ragged breath and let it out slowly. "Today I threatened that prosecutor because I was so ashamed of what my earlier behavior had caused. You may have pulled the trigger, Lauren, but I aimed the gun." Oh-so-lightly, as if fearing rejection, she touched my arm. "If you'd trusted me enough to share your suspicions, I could have prevented McIntire's last violent outburst. But you didn't, and rightfully so. It was my fault that you had to shoot him, and for that, I'm truly sorry."

I put my hand over hers and squeezed. Although I didn't actually feel anything, I had the good sense to fake the proper facial expressions and body language. Even Konstantin seemed to buy the act, and Colleen Malloy certainly did. She'd said the two hardest words to speak in any language—*I'm sorry*—and reminded me that I had obligations of my own.

Our second stop that day was Humana Hospital's

intensive care unit, where Jack McIntire eked out his slow recovery. A carefully coifed volunteer with an armful of bangle bracelets called the nurse's station, requesting permission for us to visit and assuring whoever had answered her call that we'd produced a bona fide okay from Special Agent Colleen Malloy of the FBI. After a quick exchange, she hung up the phone and explained that our patient was sleeping. Following a megadose of Konstantin's Russian charm, she picked up the phone again and managed to persuade the gatekeeper at the other end that a peek for my reassurance wouldn't violate visitor protocol.

I crept up to the sliding door in Jack McIntire's room. He sprawled across the bed, pillows propped under his shoulders and a sheet barely draping his hips. A surprisingly small bandage rode atop the mound of bruised and swollen flesh of his belly, and a small clear tube snaked from under that white square, draining the wound. I'd given him that wound, one he no doubt justly deserved, but still I felt nothing. No satisfaction. No remorse. Rather I surveyed the scene with an almost clinical detachment. Electrodes puckered the skin of his chest, and wires ran back to a bank of blinking, buzzing and beeping machines. Another tube carried oxygen to his nose and a third dripped a solution into his arm. But his chest rose and fell in a regular peaceful rhythm, and the monitor on his heart showed a strong and steady beat.

After studying him for a few minutes, I turned to the nurse's station centered in the large white room and asked one of the nurses if I could leave him a written message. At her curt nod, I scrawled two words on the back of one of my business cards. "I'm sorry." What more could I possibly say?

Back home in Eagle River, I shrugged out of my blazer, kicked off my pumps and retreated to my office. Centered squarely on my desk, my answering machine blinked and beckoned. Although I already knew that my boss had generated most of the messages, I couldn't resist the urge to count. Ten, eleven, twelve—four calls a day like clockwork, first thing in the morning, just before lunch, just after lunch and right before quitting time. He'd even stayed on in Anchorage an extra day until Nina persuaded him that I really wasn't likely to surface for a while. Among my friends, Lauren's mental-health days are common knowledge, and by now close friends can actually gauge the blow to my endurance and predict the duration of my retreat. Although I consider Boyce Reade my friend, he's also my boss and therefore not one to whom I confess my occasional need for mandatory down time. Looked like the secret was now out.

Konstantin wandered in while I brought Boyce up to date, and I waved him to the seat behind my desk. I hiked a hip onto the far edge and ran through my visits with Colleen Malloy and Jack McIntire.

When I'd finished, he ran through the actors on his end. "Lawrence Cameron expects to see you in Washington when you get back East. Ditto Margaret Armstrong. She's doing beautifully. In fact, she admits to hoping for a ghastly scar, as she calls it. Says she'd rather have a badge of courage than a trophy-class Dall ram any day."

While I chuckled, he paused, gently clearing his throat. "I explained that you weren't likely to come East for a while, and then only for a visit. I don't think a subarctic transplant would flourish here. Washington is a southern city, after all."

I considered making a joke about man's fear of a woman with a gun but didn't quite have the heart for humor. At least I'd thought of making the quip. That was a good sign.

"Thanks, Boyce. I liked them both very much. And I will come for a visit. Soon."

As I hung up the phone, I glanced at the Russian and found something new in his eyes, a sorrow lurking amid the vitality. At the sight, my heart lurched, shattering the icy numbness that had encased me for days. I could feel again. And it hurt. A lot.

"You have to leave, don't you?" I slid off the desk, wrapping my arms across my stomach. "When?"

"Tomorrow morning." He came around the desk and, for the first time, pulled me into his arms. "But you are not to be crying, *krasavista*. Even when I am going, always I am nearby. These days Siberians and Alaskans are becoming friendly neighbors. And, I am thinking, we two are becoming even more."

Until he mentioned my weeping, I'd been unaware of the tears. For a very long time, we clung together, my tears wetting his shoulder and his murmurs soothing my pain. Pain comes in different packages—the hollow pain of an empty heart and the bursting pain of a full heart. Mine was the latter, a bittersweet pain that I never wanted to end. Somehow we'd become more than friends, and yet circumstances had robbed us of the chance to explore exactly how much more than friends we could be. Becoming, Konstantin had said. Exactly what we were to each other, or would be to each other, was not yet clear. Just as the living earth is Gaia unfolding, the bond between we two living creatures was also unfolding. And because the Russian had told me that one day he'd say goodbye to his Tatiana, he'd helped me to start saying goodbye to my Max. From that gift of friendship, we were becoming something more.

"Konstantin? Mom?"

Jake's voice echoed through the door, which immediately burst open. If he noticed our embrace, he didn't let it stop him. "You guys, come on. I've got it on the screen. Wow, Konstantin! It's pretty cool."

He led us to the corner of the family room, where Nina and Jessie had gathered at the computer desk. My daughter pointed at the screen. "The writing's all funny, Konstantin. I can't read it. What does it say?"

"It is saying, 'Greetings from Arkady Radishchev and Konstantin Zorich. And welcome to the New Siberian Experiment Station.'" He brushed a finger across the computer screen. "And here is coming much information—just click. And here is coming my electric address."

"Electronic, man." Jake rolled his eyes. *"E-mail* means electronic mail. And it works." He clicked the mouse a few times and the screen changed rapidly. "Look, Mom. There's our address: maxwell@hq. denali.org. And it takes about a second to e-mail Siberia! We just tried it."

Nina stepped back from the desk and shook her head. "That's so amazing. Really amazing. The world is getting very small."

Konstantin smiled down at me. "Always nearby, *krasavista.*"

I nodded. In the 1990s the world certainly had gotten very small. I leaned my head against the Russian's shoulder and sighed. But not nearly small enough.